SWEPT UP

SWEPT UP

A Maid in LA Mystery

HOLLY JACOBS

Ilex Books 2018
ISBN-13: 978-0-9992736-8-5
ISBN-10: 0-9992736-8-X

To Lisa and everybody at the Trixie Belden homepage! Thanks for not only noticing my homage to one of my childhood favorite characters, but for embracing Quincy and her friends! So this one is for all of you, and for everyone else who grew up with the Bobwhites!

It's also for all of Quincy's fans. Thank you, thank you for all your support!

REVIEWS:

The first Maid in LA Mystery book had reviews from my family... including a stellar endorsement by my son, "At least it's not a romance." The second book had reviews from my Duets friends (comedy writers one and all) and for the third, a holiday novella, I had some help by a few holiday characters. So it should come as no surprise that I went looking for something a bit different for the 4th book, Swept Up. In Swept Up, Quincy's first adventure, Steamed, is now a movie on the HeartMark Channel. So I thought some movie reviews were in order.

(*Fictional*) Reviews for the (*Fictional*) Mortie-winning movie Steamed, based on (the very real) book by the same name and featured in Holly Jacobs' 4th Maid in LA Mystery, **Swept Up**:

"...A factual-ish movie based on a screenplay by first time writer, Quincy Mac, a one-time almost-actress, business owner and maid who accidentally cleaned a murder scene one day. If you can follow that sentence, this is a movie for you." Hammer's Hometime Movie Reviews

"Steamed, the movie, has created a whole new genre of flicks—The Mommy Mystery. Perfect for those mommies who want a laugh. And hey, even if you don't laugh, it's a couple hours away from the kids." ~Mary's Mommy Blog

"...at least it's not a romance." ~Miles Smith, screenwriter
Quincy Mac's son

"Quincy is one of the ditziest characters I've ever watched.
Really, it takes a special class of crazy to think you'd end up
in jail for accidentally cleaning a murder scene ... now, com-
mitting the murder might be cause for worry. In retrospect,
maybe Quincy was right to be concerned." ~Rocko Bauers,
Editor, Reporter and Movie Reviewer for the Orange County
Prison Paper

TABLE OF CONTENTS

Steamed: A Maid in LA Mystery (2013)
TV Movie—119 minutes—comedy, mystery, romance

Producers: Pam Ericson and Ralph Andrews
Director: Sean Ahearn

Writer: Quincy Mac
Summary:
Quincy Mac is a maid in LA—a maid who's accidently cleaned a murder scene. Now she's a murder suspect with only one option—find the real murderer before she ends up in jail for a crime she didn't commit.

Quincy came to LA looking for fame and fortune. What she's found is infamy and misfortune.

There's a killer out there, and Quincy's going to them... or die trying.

Cast:

Quincy Mac—*Priscilla Samuels*
Detective Caleb (Cal) Parker—*Jonas Miles*
Steve Banning—*Justin Fanning*
Big G, Tony Garrakowski—*Dylan Daniels*
Tessa Compernalle—*Marilyn George*
Shannon Ball Banning—*Mellie Adams*
Shaley Banning—*Peri Smith*
Cassandra—*Kelsey Brooke*
Willy—*Zach Barns*

PROLOGUE

"OH, NO. NOT AGAIN."

CHAPTER ONE
TWO HOURS EARLIER

"SPEECH, SPEECH, SPEECH, speech," everyone in the giant tent yelled. I looked around my ex-husband Jerome's backyard. Friends and family waited for me to say something.

My future-fiancé, Cal, offered me his hand and helped me up on the table. I reached into the pockets that someday-famous designer Katelyn Campbell had made for me and pulled out a crumpled piece of paper.

"It's been almost two years since I accidentally cleaned a murder scene," I started, which made all my friends and family clap. I'm not sure that cleaning a murder scene by accident deserved applause, but I waited.

When they didn't show signs of fading away, I said, "And," very loudly. They took the hint.

"So much has changed in that time," I continued. "I'm still a mother, a daughter, a friend, a maid, a business owner. But now I'm pre-engaged to the most marvelous man on earth and I'm a very lucky amateur detective...." Cal shot me a glare, and I put my notecard down and added, "a *retired*, very lucky amateur detective. And I'm a writer, too. Frankly, it all feels surreal, especially the writer part.

1

"I wanted to give my writing teacher and mentor, Dick Macy, writing credit for his help on the script, but he said no. But like I said in my acceptance speech, I wouldn't be here without Dick's help and tutelage." I nodded at Dick and sent him a smile. He'd started out as teacher, then he was my mentor. Now, almost two years later, he was a friend. A very dear friend, and an occasional cohort.

"Dick believed in my abilities. My family and friends believed in me. The only person who ever voiced any doubts about my abilities was...me. So tonight—"

I looked at the clock and corrected myself. "Well, actually this morning—as I stand here with a Mortie Award in hand." I realized I wasn't sure where my Mortie statue had ended up, so I added, "Well, at least figuratively in hand, I want to thank all of you for your support and your belief in me. And I want to remind you all, but especially my sons," this time I nodded at my three boys. Hunter, Miles, and Eli. They were my heart.

"I want to tell you boys that dreams do come true, so dream big. And for those of us who are a bit older, I want to say it's never too late to live your dream. Even if it's a dream you barely know you have. Even if you doubt yourself and have to lean on your friends' and family's belief in you. Thank you, everyone."

Everyone clapped wildly. I resisted the urge to pinch myself just to be sure that *Steamed* really did win three Morties. One for director of a made-for-TV movie, one for costumes, and one for best original screenplay...that was mine.

I reached in the pocket on the other side of my dress— seriously, I know that Katelyn's going to make it big as a designer because she can make a dress that looks sexy in an age appropriate way and she put pockets in it—and pulled out the star-shaped sunglasses that Lottie Webber had given me twenty plus years ago when I left Erie, PA for Hollywood.

"Lottie, I finally wore them on a red carpet for you." I slipped them on again.

She laughed, as did everyone else. I'd heard the media had all commented on my glasses.

Let's face it my five-minute cameo in *Steamed* hardly made me a movie star. If you watch the scene where the movie-Quincy, Pricilla Samuels, meets the movie-Shaley, Peri, at the party, you can see me in the background. I'm standing with an older man, sipping a drink.

That five-minute cameo had been the hardest part of my agent's negotiations with the movie powers-that-be. The studio wasn't thrilled when I told them I wanted to Stan-Lee the movie and have a cameo in *Steamed*, but my agent, Deanne Simon, somehow made that part of the deal. And since I was up for a Mortie for best script, I didn't feel too bad about wearing the glasses. I wasn't a star, but I was an award—winning writer.

Deanne was currently negotiating my script for *Dusted*, a second movie based on the art heist I'd solved. I'd solved a third mystery, a very small mystery, over Christmas that same year. But that one I don't talk about. I hadn't mentioned it to Dick or Deanne because that one wasn't fodder for a script. It was personal.

I picked out a few members of the cast of *Steamed* who'd come to our after-after party. I hoped they'd all sign back on for the second movie. Pricilla Samuels, who went by Cilla to her friends, was a much better Quincy than I felt I was. I mean, I don't think she ever needed to suck in her stomach, and she managed to make my irrational fear (yes, I can acknowledge that my going to jail because I accidentally cleaned a murder scene wasn't very likely... but at the time I was terrified) about being arrested seem plausible. She was standing in the corner with her husband, Dylan. Dylan Daniels. He played Big G in the movie. Dylan and Big G shared a lot of physical characteristics. And they were both very nice guys. Just plain old if-I-had-a-daughter-I'd-be-happy-if-she-dated-them sort of guys.

Cilla spotted me and came up and hugged me. "My agent said *Dusted* is looking good. I told her I was in and she said no matter what, don't tell anyone how much I wanted to play you again or else she'd have nothing to bargain with. So don't tell, but I so want to play you again." She hugged me.

Cilla was a hugger. She was also a major actress who took the role of Quincy on the heels of her big budget movie that was coming out next year. She was playing opposite some of Hollywood's biggest names. Deanne had mentioned the producers weren't sure they could entice her back to another made for TV movie.

"I was afraid you'd feel it was a step backwards. After all you just finished that movie where you and Robert Downi—"

She cut me off. "Listen, Quincy. I'm an actress. And I love what I do. Working on *Steamed* was so much fun, and playing you was even more so. How could I say no to a chance to do it again?"

I knew exactly how she could say no. I'd been on the fringes of Hollywood for years, thanks to my marriage to producer Jerome Smith back in the day. A number of actors who *made it big* bought into their own hype. Cilla was not one of those. Neither was her husband, Dylan.

I circulated through the room. Mom and Dad both hugged me and told me how proud they were of me. Even my very stick-in-the-mud (or stick up the … well, you know) brothers hugged me. It was sort of weird but in a nice way. A lot of the cast, friends, and family came up to me as well.

After making the rounds of all the big parties we'd all come back to Jerome and Peri's, where we watched the show again.

It was seven a.m., and I thought there was a very good chance that at some point I was going to simply topple over. But I hadn't reached that point yet.

Seeing my script turned into a movie had been surreal.

But tonight, watching it win awards—watching me win an award—that was even more surreal. Surrealer?

I'd made my speech in my Katelyn Campbell designer gown, and though it was as comfortable as a gown could be, I was ready for this Cinderella to turn back into herself. And I'd thought ahead and left a bag in Hunter's room here at his dad's.

I headed for the stairs and practically bumped into a rock-hard ox of a man. "Sorry," I said.

"No problem, Ms. Mac."

"I'm sorry. Do I know you?"

He shook his head. "Security, ma'am."

He looked very secret-servicey in his dark suit and dark glasses. Leave it to Peri to decide we needed security. "Congratulations," he said.

"Thank you." I went upstairs and used Hunter's room to change. I looked glam for an entire evening. That's all I could manage.

As I changed into jeans and a comfy sweatshirt that had a Mac'Cleaner's logo on it, I decided I was much more comfortable with the behind the scenes part of movie making than in front of the camera. If I had to be glam and put-together on a regular basis... well, I don't think I could pull it off.

There was a knock on the door. "I'm in here."

"It's Cal."

"Come on in." He opened the door and I realized that here was someone who was glam and put together without even trying. He looked great no matter what he wore, but I'll confess, in a tux, he looked hot. And totally kissable.

I walked into his arms and kissed him.

Yep. I was right.

Totally kissable.

"What was that for?" he asked, then added, "Not that I'm complaining."

"That was just because you're you, and I love you."

He pulled the engagement ring I'd had around my neck for a bit more than a year. When I married Jerome all those years ago, I'd been swept away. I'd come to Hollywood with a dream of acting, and I'd swept that dream under the rug for romance and it stayed under the rug after my divorce while Tiny and I built our cleaning business.

Now, I'm not saying that sometimes love isn't worth changing your dream for, but maybe true love doesn't make you change, it just makes you better, stronger. That's how I felt about Cal. I'd been swept up by him as well, but rather than make me change, he'd made me better. When he asked me to marry him and I asked for time, he'd understood. Hence our almost-engaged status.

I leaned my head against him.

"Are we ready to make it official?" he asked, still toying with the ring on the chain.

"I've been thinking about that."

He leaned down and nibbled at my neck. "And?" he asked between nibbles.

"And what?"

Here's the thing, when Cal's nibbling or kissing, or …whatever he's doing. When he's doing it, I find it hard to think. Frankly, I sometimes find it hard to breathe. Even now, I still find it amazing he's mine. Whether the ring was around my neck or on my finger, he was indeed mine just as I was his.

He laughed. "You were thinking about this..." he prompted as he gave a gentle tug on the chain.

"Oh. How about in August we get officially engaged? On our two—year anniversary of when we met."

"Quincy, you do realize we met at murder scene?" he asked, as if I needed reminded.

Even almost two years later, I still shivered at the thought. "I do. But I count our anniversary when we met outside the murder scene, so we basically met on a street. You looked so handsome as you walked toward me. I thought you saw me looking cute and vulnerable. I didn't realize you thought I was a suspect."

"I never thought—"

This was an old argument. I was trying to be romantic and didn't want to rehash it. "Shh. That moment, when you walked over to me, I had a feeling there was something there. At least on my part. That moment, that's what I consider our meeting. I'm not counting when you interrogated me as part of it."

He shook his had. "You are so weird."

"Lucky you like weird."

He laughed again. "Yeah, it is."

I started to move back into his arms, but he shook his head. "We're in your ex-husband's house, in your son's room. One quick make-out session is all I can manage."

I took a step back. "You're right. But later, at home..."

He nodded. "Later."

I left my bag and dress on the hanger in Hunter's room. There were other bags there. I come from comfortable folk—people more apt to wear jeans than haute couture.

After Cal changed, we went back downstairs and out back. My friend Honey had insisted that her restaurant, *Psst*, cater a breakfast. Mimosas, quiches, pastries, coffee.... It was wonderful.

I noticed that Honey and Big G, Cal's best friend, were looking all chummy at a table. I saw Cassandra, who I'd met because of that original dead body, and Julian, who I'd met as I investigated the art heist, were sitting together with my best friend and business partner, Tiny and her husband, Sal. They still acted like newlyweds.

I took Cal's hand. I understood how Tiny felt about Sal now. There was a sense of completeness when I was with Cal.

I saw Peri, talking to my mom. I loved they'd become so close. Jerome was talking to Mellie Adams.

I did a double-take.

Mellie Adams? Bleck.

There was no way Peri invited her, and I was certain that I hadn't invited her. I couldn't think of anyone on the set who would have suggested that she join us.

Which meant she was crashing.

I couldn't believe she'd had the gall to crash my party tonight—or this morning. She was the most obnoxious woman I'd ever worked with. I'd visited the movie set one day and she'd shouted for me to go get her a bottle of water, like I was her maid. Well, I was a maid, but I wasn't *her* maid.

Mellie played Shannon Ball Banning, a very secondary part in the movie. One of dead Mr. Banning's exes. Shannon hadn't been very endearing, but Mellie was so much more obnoxious.

It wasn't just me who had a problem with her. Pretty much everyone on the set did. From Sean, the director, to Cilla who played me. It seems Mellie thought that lead role should have been hers. She did her best to sabotage Cilla whenever they had a scene together. I hadn't liked Shannon in real life, and I liked Mellie even less.

"You're growling," Lottie said.

I turned around and hugged my childhood best friend. "I'm so glad you were able to be here."

"Quincy, I wouldn't have missed it for the world. I just wanted to say goodbye. I've got a one o'clock flight and I need to stop at the hotel, change and grab my stuff. I just wanted to say how proud I am of you. Everyone in Erie is. Did you see *GoErie.com* this morning?"

GoErie.com was my hometown, Erie, Pennsylvania's newspaper's online site. I shook my head.

"You're the top story," she said excitedly. "Front page, above the fold. I'll send you a couple actual paper copies when I get home."

I hugged her again. "I'm so glad you came."

"You've built a good life for yourself here in LA, Quincy. I loved meeting your friends. And I love that you not only kept those silly star-shaped glasses all these years, but that you wore them on the red carpet."

"You believed in me, Lottie. I can't tell you how much that meant to me when I first got out here. I was alone, and though I'd never admit it, I was afraid. Those glasses were a tangible sign that someone believed in me. They were a talisman of sort."

I am not a hugger but Lottie is, so we hugged.

"And thank you for never saying anything about—" she started.

I shushed her. She didn't need to finish. I knew what she was talking about. It was a tiny little mystery I'd solved on a Christmas visit. A mystery I'd never write about or mention, but in my head I called it *Spruced Up*. It sort of fit with the other two titles.

"The money you donated made a big difference," she whispered. "Thank you again."

I saw Lottie out and went back into the tent that filled up Jerome and Peri's backyard. I looked out over everyone in the crowd. My three boys were in a corner with my parents, brothers, and their wives who'd come in from Erie, Pennsylvania.

Friends. Old friends. New friends. They filled the tent.

Lottie was right. I'd built a very good life for myself in LA.

A happy life.

I was a very lucky woman.

At about nine a.m. people finally had partied enough. They left in groups. My family left, too. They were going to the hotel to change, then straight to the airport. Let's face it, the fact all six of them were doctors meant that my hometown couldn't do without them for long.

My three boys, Hunter, Miles, and Eli hugged me before they left to go back to their college dorms. College boys are not normally big huggers, especially when their mother isn't a hugger by nature. I got a bit misty.

Hunter said, "We're so proud of you, Mom."

I moved from misty to teary in a literal blink of the eye. The boys were all a year apart. Hunter had just turned twenty and the other boys had birthdays soon. They'd be nineteen and eighteen. Yes, soon all my kids would be legal adults. The thought was unsettling.

I'd thought I'd have this entire year with just Eli at home, but he'd finished his high school credits, graduated over the holidays, and started college after the holidays.

I had an empty nest sooner than expected. And I'd told Cal I wanted the experience of being on my own, but these few months seemed long enough. Yes, by August I'd be more than ready to be officially engaged.

The boys had barely left my hug when Peri ran up and hugged all three of them. "Now you all be good, but not too good," she teased.

The boys all laughed.

Some mothers would be intimidated if their ex-husband's new wife was on good terms with her kids, but not me … not with Peri. I mean, she landed the role of Shaley in the movie. That meant she was playing a teenager even though she was in her twenties. I remember my twenties and my teens in a distant sort of way. I certainly couldn't play a teen or even a twenty year old in a movie.

But I couldn't resent the fact Peri played a teenager because Peri is … Peri. Not liking Peri would be like not liking Santa Claus.

Or kittens.

Or rainbows.

My mother had tried not to like her, and generally when Judith Quincy Mac set her mind to something she succeeded. Except with not liking Peri. Mom admitted failure in short order and now they were friends.

After the boys left, Peri said, "Listen, you don't have to be the last man standing. You just go home and I'll see everyone else out."

"But I thought I'd wait and help clean up."

"Quincy, this was your party. The guest of honor—the Mortie Award winning writer—doesn't clean up after her own party."

"But—" I tried to interrupt, but Peri interrupted my interruption. "Even if you are a maid by trade. Tonight, or this morning, you're an award-winning writer. Go home and try to get some sleep."

"Let me just get my things." Before I could turn around, Peri hugged me, too.

"I'm so proud of you," she said. "And I'm so thrilled that my first real acting credit was in your movie."

I'd often joked that when Jerome divorced her—Jerome always divorces his wives before they hit twenty-five—I was going to adopt her. Only it wasn't really a joke. The boys, my mom, and I had decided that Peri was family.

We all know that family isn't about blood...it's about love. So no matter what, we were keeping Peri.

I hadn't realized just how exhausted I was. I dragged myself upstairs to get Cal's and my stuff.

I opened the door to Hunter's room.

"Oh, no. Not again."

CHAPTER TWO

"OH, NO. NOT AGAIN," I said a second time as I stood in the doorway and looked in the room.

And for a moment, time stood still.

Then the next moment, time rewound and I was standing in Mr. Banning's house. I'd just opened his door and found him dead on his bed.

That moment had derailed my life. It had totally pivoted the direction I was moving in.

And now....

I slammed back into the present and there, on Hunter's bed—on my son's bed here at his father's house—was another dead body.

Don't ask me how I knew Mellie Adams was dead. The fact that her eyes were wide open, but she wasn't moving was one reason. The fact her face was deathly white was another—I guess there's a reason they refer to that kind of pallor as deathly white. But really it was whatever had made Mellie *Mellie* was gone.

That's when I noticed something other than Mellie being dead. Her dead hands were clutching...a Mortie award.

And that's when my moment of deja vu muddleness gave way to the horror of the scene in front of me. And I did what any sane woman would...I screamed.

I screamed a girly scream.

I screamed shrill, long, and loud.

I screamed for I don't know how long, but I finally stopped when I heard footsteps.

"Quince, what the hell?" Cal said as he pulled me into his arms.

"She's dead."

"Who—" he started to ask, then stopped as he saw for himself who.

"Not again," he said.

"That's exactly what I said," I told him.

"Did you go in the room?"

"No."

"Good. No one goes in that room until the authorities arrive." He reached in far enough to grab the door hand and shut the door.

He pulled his phone out of his pocket and dialed.

I didn't point out that he was part of the authorities.

And then I realized if he was here in the house where a dead body was discovered then he wasn't a cop in this case… he was a suspect.

So was everyone who'd been at the party.

And everyone who was here was a friend or a loved one.

People came up the stairs to see what was going on, but Cal waved them away. He said something. I couldn't seem to follow what those words were as the weight of what this meant sank in.

Mellie was dead in Peri's house. In my son's room. In my son's bed. I'd seen her alive when she arrived, which means she was killed sometime during the party. A party where my friends and family were all guests.

That meant everyone I loved would be considered a suspect.

I'm not sure if Cal dialed 911, or called the station directly. I could see him talking on the phone but I'm not sure what he said. I think he waved more people away. I'm not sure.

It was as if all the sound around me went watery. Like I was in the deep end of a pool and someone was talking to me from the diving board. I knew Cal was saying things to me, but I couldn't make out what.

I'd figured out who killed Mr. Banning because I was terrified I'd go to prison for a crime I didn't commit... but had cleaned.

I figured out who stole paintings from our clients and replaced them with forgeries in order to save my business, Mac'Cleaner's, reputation.

I'd figured out who stole supplies from my parents' practice in order to please my mother... maybe I did it to prove, that although I wasn't a doctor like everyone else in the family, I had talents. But I'd never told anyone that I'd solved that particular mystery, though my mother guessed.

But this time the stakes were much higher than saving myself, or saving my business, or pleasing my mother.

This time I had to find the real killer because someone I love might end up being wrongly accused.

Now when *Steamed* came out on the HeartMark channel, a few of the negative reviews referred to my character in the movie as 'ditzy.' They scoffed at the idea of anyone worrying they'd be convicted of a murder they didn't commit but merely had cleaned.

But here's the thing, my Uncle Bill, the only other non-doctor in the family, had gone to jail for a crime he didn't commit. Eventually he was released but not until after he'd gotten a tattoo.

Macs do not get tattoos.

They don't go to prison, even if they're simply wrongly accused and convicted.

I felt sick thinking about the cops coming to my parents' hospital and dragging my mother out of surgery and taking her to jail.

My mother would not survive prison. Or my father, my brothers or my sisters-in-law.

Or what if the cops suspected my boys?

The images of friends who'd come to the party to support me, friends who would now be considered suspects ran through my mind like a slideshow. Tiny. Sal. Peri. Big G... Heck even Theresa, the worst employee in the history of Mac'Cleaners.

Well, she used to be the worst employee, but once I got involved with the movie, I'd stepped back on the day-to-day operations and Theresa started to do more office work and it turned out she was wonderful at that. She was dating my computer guru resource, Rob, now. What about him? I don't know if he'd survive in a cell with no computer and no internet.

Why was I thinking about Theresa and Rob when Mellie Adams was dead in my son's bed?

At some point I must have sat down because I was on the floor in Jerome's hall because Cal was kneeling next to me.

"Quince, come on. Pull it together."

"Okay, Cal." I said the words, but I wasn't sure I could manage to follow through.

He kissed me. "It will be all right."

"Will it? Because from where I'm sitting—from where I'm literally sitting—it looks like a total wreck. It's been more than a year since anything even remotely mysterious happened. I thought I was done with dead bodies and art heists. And yet, here I am, on a night that should have been one of the highlights of my life, and there's a dead freakin' body in my son's bed. The body of the meanest-spirited woman I ever met. Figuring out who wanted to kill Mellie Adams is going to be difficult because everyone who ever met that woman wanted to kill her at one time or another."

"Quincy, you can't say things like that."

"Really? You think whoever investigates this won't realize she was an awful woman and everyone who worked with her on this movie wanted to strangle her at least once... once a day, if not more often? I don't think anyone, even the actors from the movie, are good enough at acting to sell that."

He sighed. "I know. I talked to her tonight, this morning. Peri asked me to ask her to leave. She wasn't invited, you know."

"Oh, I know." Then I realized what he was saying. "When did you talk to her?"

"About an hour ago." He paused a moment, then said, "And afterward, I saw her go upstairs. I assumed she was getting her things."

"Oh." I let the ramification of his statement sink in. There was a good chance Cal had been one of the last people to see Mellie alive.

"Did you see her come back down?"

"No. I started talking to Big G and Honey," he said. "I remembering thinking they seemed perfect together. And then I thought about how much you'd like that."

"Quincy, you need to get out of here," Peri said as she crested the stairway. "I told you, I'd take care of seeing everyone else out."

"Peri," Cal said, "You can't let anyone leave. I'd appreciate it if you asked everyone who's still here to wait for a few minutes. We have a slight problem."

"What kind of problem? Is everything all right?"

17

"I—"

And Cal seemed unable to find the words to tell her.

Peri was sweetness personified. How was she going to cope with knowing someone died in her house?

I used to own this house. My sons still stayed here on a regular basis. And I knew I was never going to think about this house the same way.

And as I had that thought I felt guilty because I wasn't mourning Mellie. But really, who would? I was upset that this had happened here. That it was going to impact my friends and family. That it was going to taint this house I used to call home, and now Peri called home.

"Peri—" I started to tell her, but Cal grabbed my arm and shook his head.

"We'll be down in a few minutes and fill everyone in. A few cops are coming—"

"Are your friends coming to congratulate Quincy? I wish you would have said something. I'd have put them on the guest list. I'll just keep everyone who's still here here…if that makes sense." And with a laugh she bolted down the stairs before I could stop her.

"We should tell her," I said.

"No. We can't leave the room unattended and it would be best if no one knows that we found the body. If the killer is here we want him or her to stay here."

I nodded.

That's when it really sank in…the killer had been in this house.

Odds were that they were an invited guest. Someone I knew. Maybe someone I loved.

It had been over a year since I felt I needed to use my white-board. But I had a feeling I'd be dragging it out of storage and setting it up again when I got home.

I glanced at Cal.

I knew he'd tell me not to meddle. He'd tell me to trust that his friends, whoever was assigned to the case, would figure out who killed Mellie Adams.

And I knew that I couldn't do that. I couldn't trust the lives of people I loved to anyone but myself.

I was sure my writing mentor, Dick Macy, would be thrilled that I'd found myself thick in the midst of another mystery.

That made one of us.

CHAPTER THREE

D ETECTIVE CHARLES RANDOLPH was a long, slow sip of cold water on a hot summer's day. That's what Grandma Mac would have said. And in this case, I'd have to agree with her.

Now, I know I'm almost engaged, but being almost engaged doesn't mean I couldn't appreciate a work of art when I spotted one.

Detective Charlie was that and then some.

He was tall, lean, and had intense eyes. Dark, short hair that was temptingly thick. It made a woman want to run her fingers through it.

He was also a very good listener.

He had me tell him in minute detail what had happened. He listened intently as I tried to go back over it.

Then he asked about the party itself, who was there. What I remembered of Mellie's arrival.

I decided honesty was the best policy. I recounted everything I remembered. Mellie arrived. She made the rounds. I was not pleased. And I noticed no one else seemed overjoyed to see her. "And I'm not talking about just the movie crew, I'm talking about everyone. Mellie has—had—a *way* about her. She acted as if she was superior to everyone. From my parents, to the cast, to the crew, to my friends.

Even the catering staff wore the exact same expression after they'd endured Mellie's attention."

"What expression was that?" he asked.

"Have you ever asked for something and got something totally different? For instance, I had a friend from Japan back in high school—an exchange student. Her family put sugar on their popcorn. The first time we went to the movies together, she grabbed a handful of popcorn. There was shock and distaste on her face. Or, when my mom and I went to Canada and she asked for iced tea. Now, if we're down south, we know to ask if it's sweet tea or unsweetened. But Canada is more north than Erie and it seemed like they shouldn't have sweet tea. But turns out, that's all they have. My mom—my very prim and proper mom—took a drink and got that same look and then she snorted tea out her nose.

"That's the look people get when Mellie breezed by them. She's—she *was*—a beautiful woman. They expected her to be as sweet as she looked. They got that look when they realized she was not."

"So no one liked her." Randolph made it more a statement then a question.

"No one. I could lie to you, but I find it's best to avoid lying to the cops."

"And you've had a lot of experience with that, haven't you?" He gave me a look that said he knew all about my other brush-ups with the cops. Of course, since the movie, even people who didn't hear about Mr. Banning's murder at the time knew about it now.

"I—" I had no idea how to answer that question. I'd never really lied to cops. Not to Cal or Mickey Roman, who investigated the missing paintings. But I hadn't been exactly forthright. I could have shared more of my own investigation with them.

Charlie—it made me feel more at ease to think of him as Charlie, rather than Detective Randolph—set his notebook down and looked at me in that intense way of his. "Quincy—may I call you Quincy?"

I nodded. It seemed fair since I was calling him Charlie in my mind.

"I'm from a different precinct than Cal, but I know him by reputation, and frankly every cop in LA knows about you."

I sighed. The fact that every cop in LA knew about me was not a good thing.

"I will confess," he continued, "that I wasn't thrilled when I caught this case because I knew you'd be part of the package. And I want to assure you that I'm going to find out who killed Ms. Adams. My first instinct was to tell you I wouldn't hesitate to put you in jail if you interfered with my case. But I've seen your movie, and I talked to Roman on my way over. He called to warn me about you. He told me he'd tried threatening you with obstruction charges and jail. He also told me his threats didn't do sh … squat. So I've changed my mind about how I'm going to handle you."

I started to protest I didn't need handled, but Charlie held up his hand. "I'm going to talk to everyone who's still here. Your sons' stepmother—" He picked up his notebook.

"Peri," I filled in for him.

"Yes, Peri. She's getting me a guest list, and I'll be calling people who had already left and set up interviews. I'm going to find who killed Ms. Adams. And I suspect you're already thinking about doing the same thing. But rather than warn you off—and stressing that I'm not encouraging you to investigate on your own and I'll be thrilled if you tell me that you'll leave it to me—but having at least a glimmer of how your mind works, I'm going to ask you to share anything you find with me. I promise I'll take it seriously. You already showed a willingness to do that when you told me no one liked Ms. Adams."

I studied the man sitting across from me. Maybe thinking of him as Charlie had made me warm to him. Or maybe after being with Cal for almost two years, I'd realized cops were like everyone else. Some were wonderful, some not so much. Most were genuinely good guys who got into the profession in order to help people. I thought Charlie was one of those ... a good guy.

So I nodded. "You're not going to dismiss my observations out of hand?"

"I am not."

"Well, then can I tell you something that's struck me as I went over things with you? I'm not really sure what it means. And it's definitely more of an opinion than a fact."

This time he was the one who nodded.

"Someone wants you to look at me. I'm not sure that they want you to suspect me, but they want you to think about the movie, or about what happened to me in real life. Mellie was holding a Mortie. Do you know whose?"

I didn't want to be selfish but a part of me—a small part that I hate admitting to—didn't want it to be mine. My memories of this night would be tainted enough without my actual award being used as Mellie's murder weapon.

"I can't share much about my active investigation, but I can't imagine there's a problem with me asking you where you left yours?" he said.

"I've been trying to figure that out. I think the last time I saw it, Peri had put it on the mantle."

"Then I suspect if you go look, you'd still find it there."

He was telling me the Mortie that Mellie was holding wasn't mine.

Good. Although I did feel smaller for having asked and a bit smaller yet for the huge wave of relief that it wasn't mine. "Can you tell me whose it was?"

"Not yet. When I feel I can, I will. Listen, I can't really work *with* you. That's not how homicide cops do things. We don't share with the public."

I snorted and despite the horrific circumstances, I laughed. "Cal doesn't share anything. I think he's afraid I've got a taste for investigating and if he tells me the least little thing about his cases I'll try to help. But I don't have a taste for investigating. I just love my family and friends. When they're at risk, I feel I have to do something."

"Because of your Uncle Bill," he said.

From that statement, I knew he'd really paid attention to the movie. My Uncle Bill had felt like a star, even though he was just referred to, not portrayed in the movie. He came out and stayed with me when the movie first aired on HeartMark Channel. Peri had a party then, too. He'd loved being a minor celebrity—a man who went to prison for a crime he didn't commit. He showed off his prison tattoo all night.

He hadn't come out for this party, but he'd called. I'd been disappointed he couldn't make it, but now I was relieved. The last thing Uncle Bill needed was to be a suspect.

"Yes, because of Uncle Bill. He spent years in prison for a crime he didn't commit. I don't know you. I don't know how to trust you to figure out who killed Mellie. I don't know how to trust you with my friends and family."

He considered that a moment. "What about Cal? I mean, if I screw up, I know he'd work on it."

"I love Cal." Even after a year and a half of saying the words, they still gave me an odd thrill. I loved him. We were not go-out-and-party people. We were hang-out-on-the-couch-and-watch-a-show sort of people. We were sit-next-to-each-other-at-the-table-and-work-on-our-own-jobs-together sort of people. We were even go-out-with-friends, or go-out-with-my-boys sort of people.

It was the simple things together that made us happy. I guess I loved those simple things about him.

I loved how he could shoot me a look, and I would immediately know what he was thinking.

I loved that when he slept over, I'd get up and start the coffee, and more often than not, he'd get up in time to bring me a cup. There's something so sweet about him waiting on me like that.

I love the way he fit in with my boys. He didn't try to father them but simply tried to be a friend. When they were all together something in me melted every time.

I love the way he supported my writing. Then the movie.

I just love him.

And I'd trust him with my life.

But I didn't have it in me to sit back and trust that he'd figure it out, even if I loved him and trusted him. That might not make sense. It might make me as *ditzy* as the movie reviewers claimed. But I wasn't a sit back and let someone else take care of things sort of person.

"I love Cal, and I trust that he'd look for who did it…but I'd still feel like I had to look, too. They're *my* friends. *My* family. Mellie died in my ex-husband and Peri's house…a house I used to own. She died in my son's room. No, I don't have it in me to sit back and just let other people handle it. Not even Cal."

When I was younger and married to Jerome, I might have done just that—trusted someone else to take care of a problem. But after Jerome and I divorced I'd had to

learn to stand on my own two feet. I was raising three boys
and couldn't call Jerome every time I had a problem. I was
starting a business, and though Tiny was a great partner, I
couldn't run to her with every snag. I learned to depend on
myself. I had others to support and help, but ultimately, I
relied on me.

"Here's what I'm going to do," Charlie said. "I'll share
what I can, when I can. And you share what you find with
me. I won't go all Roman on you and threaten to send you
to jail for interfering with my investigation."

"Detective Roman was a pain in my a… butt." Even
under these kind of conditions I avoided swearing. "I appreciate your working with me. You've got a deal."

"And Quincy, I'd prefer it if you stayed out of this
entirely." He paused and must have seen something in my
expression because he sighed and said, "But since I don't see
that happening, I just want to say, be careful. You're right.
The Mortie says something. Something that ties to that first
murder you solved, or maybe to the movie, or maybe simply
to you. Any of those are reason enough for me to say be
careful, but in addition, I know you won't stay out of it, so
that's even more reason. Be careful. Stay safe. I don't know
Cal well, but I know him well enough to know that he'll
never forgive either of us if you get hurt."

I thrust out a hand. "I promise, I will."

Detective Charlie shook it.

I went out into front yard, where the party-goers were
congregated. Cal hurried to my side. Tiny and Sal were right
behind him. Then Peri. … A whole gang of people gathered
around me. Charlie called Jonas Miles, who'd played Cal
in the movie, into the study. As soon as the door shut, the
questions started ringing out. From *what happened?* and *are
you investigating.* There was one rather loud *good riddance.* I

didn't see who said that one, but I knew just about everyone at the party agreed.

I faced them all and said, "Listen, everyone. We can't talk about what happened here tonight until after we've all talked to the detective. We don't want to taint each other's memories."

Dick called out, "But will you be looking into it?"

Cal stepped forward and glared at me. I knew what he wanted me to say, but I wasn't going to lie to Dick or anyone else, so I nodded. "Yes. I'll be calling everyone after the detective is done interviewing all of us."

I could see Dick's excitement. Deanne, my agent—who was also Dick's agent—was working on that deal for *Dusted*. Her eyes lit up. I didn't need to be an agent to know that a third true-life mystery would be her dream. If I could figure this out.

That was a big *if*, as far as I was concerned.

Cal grabbed my arm and pulled me away from the crowd, not roughly, but with purpose.

"Quince—" he started.

"Listen, before you start, Charlie—"

"Charlie?" he said.

"Detective Charles Randolph. If I call him Charlie it puts us on even footing," I told him. "Anyway, Charlie and I already talked. I'm not going to interfere with his investigation, *and....*" I put emphasis on that and. "I am going to share anything I find with him, and he's going to share what he can with me. I promised him I'd be careful and...."

Cal pulled me into his arms and kissed me. He kissed me hard and long. "Listen you crazy, infuriating woman, I wasn't going to scold you."

"You weren't?"

"No. I know—just like Randolph obviously knows—that you're going to do what you're going to do, whether I like it or not. But Quincy, this one's dangerous. Whoever murdered Mellie Adams wanted the cops looking at you."

I nodded. "Yes. That's what I said to Charlie. I think whoever killed Mellie put the Mortie there with purpose. I don't think it was the murder weapon. I didn't see any blood, and her head didn't look bashed in like Mr. Bannings." It was sad that I knew what a bashed in head looked like.

"I think it's a distraction," I continued. "The killer wants the cops looking at me and at my family, or at the movie in order to distract everyone from them and his-or-her motives."

"The killer has already proved he-or-she is dangerous."

"I know. I promise I'll be careful. I—"

"*We.*" This time he gave a word emphasis.

"We?" I didn't understand.

"Yes, you and me. I've talked to the Chief and I'm taking some personal time. I've banked a lot of vacation, so it's not a problem. I'm taking time off and *we* are going to look into this together. Well, I can't really look into another cop's investigation, but I'm going to follow you around as you look into it."

I must have looked as confused as I felt because Cal said, "I'm not going to try and talk you out of it. I'm not going to try to convince you to trust Randolph. He seems like a good cop. I made some calls and asked around and he's well respected. But I'm not willing to trust even the best cop with our friends and family."

I melted.

We.

Our.

Our friends and family.

I toyed with the engagement ring I still wore around my neck. When Cal had proposed to me the Christmas before last, I told him I loved him and I wanted to marry him. But I needed time. Time to stand on my own two feet. Time to figure out who I was and what I wanted.

He gave me that time.

I'd mentioned making our engagement official on our anniversary, but suddenly waiting that long seemed silly. I didn't need time to know who I was—who I was was better when Cal was with me. And I didn't need time to know what I wanted. I looked at the man standing next to me and knew without a doubt just what I wanted.

I unhooked the clasp on the gold chain and slid the ring off.

Cal didn't say anything. He simply watched as I took the ring and handed it to him. "Cal, will you ask me again to marry you?"

He grinned and sank to one knee. "Quincy Mac, will you marry me?"

I took the ring, slid it on my finger, and practically knocked him over as I threw myself into his arms and cried out, "Yes."

With my sparkly ring in place on my finger and our kissing done, I looked at him and said, "So after *we* figure out who killed Mellie Adams, we'll start to plan a wedding." I was thinking something small and intimate, but I had a feeling Tiny and my Mom wouldn't be thinking that at all.

I refused to worry about that now. I kissed my fiancé— no almost about it.

It might not be the way most people would want to start their official engagement, but it seemed appropriate for us.

CHAPTER FOUR

A FTER CHARLIE FINISHED interviewing everyone who was still at the party, we finally left Jerome's house, which was now a crime scene.

My ex said he'd get a hotel with Peri until the house was cleared and they could go back.

I insisted they come stay with me.

Now, I know most people wouldn't invite their ex and his current wife to stay at their home. But Peri is one of my best friends, and Jerome and I—

Well, we'd established we were better off co-parenting than being married. We'd become friendly over the years. It worked for us.

Tiny and Sal came over, too. There are times when a woman needs to be surrounded by friends—this was one of those times.

I'd asked Dick over as well, but he had a meeting with some media muckety muck about his new show—*Every Body, Inc.* He offered to cancel, but let's face it, there wasn't anything he could do, so I sent him on his way. But while I was delighted about how well his show was doing, I did notice the irony of the title, given the fact I'd found yet another body.

On our drive home, I called the boys—thankful they'd left before we found Mellie—and filled them in on what was going on. "Not again, Mom," was pretty much the gist of Miles and Eli's response. And Hunter said something like that, then added, "Gross. Just for the record, I'm switching rooms."

"I'll tell your dad," I promised.

"And I want new furniture."

"I don't blame you," I said.

Jerome's house had eight bedrooms, so it wouldn't be a huge problem for him to let Hunter move into another one.

I told each of the boys I'd like them to write down everything they remembered from the party—even the most minute detail could make a difference. They said they'd e-mail me their lists. After I hung up with them, I called my mom's phone and left a voice message.

By the time we got home, it was lunch.

Before I found Mellie, I'd planned on going to bed and spending the day there, but I was too wound up for that now. So I ordered pizzas and we sat around and went over everything again.

"Quincy, where's your white-board?" Tiny asked.

I used a white-board like one of my television detective heroine's when I looked for Mr. Banning's murderer, then again when I tried to figure out who'd stolen clients' paintings and replaced them with forgeries. I used it in that small Christmas mystery I don't talk about.

My white-board had been a star in and of itself in the movie. The scene where Cilla, playing me, tried to get it in the house was comedic genius. That's not me being cocky about my writing, but rather me paying homage to Cilla's acting talents.

My white-board was tucked up in the shed out back with the boys' bikes, skis, and other sports equipment. I thought that's where it would stay. To be honest, I didn't—and don't—have any interest in becoming a professional amateur sleuth.

But it seems my intentions didn't matter. Here I was, back in the thick of it again.

Cal and Jerome went out to the shed and hauled the white-board back inside.

This time, rather than being relegated to a bedroom, we set it up in the living room.

I didn't need to try to hide the white-board from Cal this time. Nor did I have to hide the fact I was going to look for Mellie's murderer.

I watched Cal clean the dust of the board and felt my heart melt just a bit.

I know, I know, I sound like a romance novel with phrases like *my-heart-melted*, but there it was. It did.

There were so many things about Cal I loved. I just added the fact that he believed in me and he was helping me find the murderer to the list.

After the white-board was set up and Cal was sitting next to me, the six of us went to town. Peri gave us a copy of her guest list. Then we went online to NMD (Net Movie Data) and pulled info and pictures on everyone who was in the industry. My printer went full-speed and as a backup, I sent copies of everyone's pictures to my cellphone. I figured I'd have them on hand if I needed them. Then we put pictures and pertinent info on everyone up on the white-board.

Everyone talked and, in a weird way, seemed to enjoy working together to compile the information. But once it was together, we stared at the board and the room got quiet, except for the sound of serial yawning. One person would start one, and slowly the yawn would work its way through all of us.

We stared, serial yawned, and got nowhere.

Frankly, we were all running on fumes.

"This is ridiculous," I finally said. "None of us has slept since night before last. We're not going to get anywhere this way. Let's call it a night."

My ring must have caught Tiny's eye because she squealed and grabbed my hand. Then Peri joined her. Sal and Jerome took a step back.

"When?" Tiny asked.

"Tell us everything," Peri commanded.

"While Cal and I were waiting for Charlie to finish the interviews at your house, I realized that life was short and I didn't want to be without him, so—"

"Wait, are you telling me you finally made your engagement official at a murder scene?" Tiny asked.

I nodded. It seemed romantic at the time, but when she put it like that, it didn't.

The engagement news took some time to play out. Peri and Tiny were already discussing my wedding plans. I shot Cal a help-me look. He just shifted closer to Jerome and Sal.

Cowards.

"Really, we all need to get some sleep," I said.

They both did stop, much to my surprise.

Tiny hugged me. "I'm so sorry that you're in the middle of something like this again. This shouldn't have happened to you. It was your night. The press is going to have a field day."

I groaned. "They definitely are."

"Don't come into the office," Tiny continued. "Theresa and I will manage everything there. And when you get calls, we'll take names and numbers. You should probably think about talking to someone in the media. Throw the press a bone. And maybe you can find a way to make the press work for you. I've been reading JD Robb's series, and her heroine has one reporter friend she works with all the time. Maybe you need to cultivate a reporter."

I didn't plan on being involved in another investigation after this, so I didn't need to cultivate anyone.

But I said, "That's a good idea. Maybe I'll talk to Charlie and see if there's someway I can use the press coverage to help the investigation."

Sal hugged me next. "Don't do anything illegal, and if you do, don't get caught. But if you do get caught, call me immediately and don't say anything until I get there."

I leaned down and kissed his cheek.

Peri and Jerome went to bed in Hunter's room.

Cal and I were finally alone in the living room. I waved my glittery ringed hand at him. "No second thoughts?"

"About marrying you or about working on this with you?" he asked.

"Both or either," I said.

"No doubts at all."

We sat on the couch and he wrapped his arm around me.

It felt like coming home.

I stared at the white-board.

"I didn't think I'd ever do this again. Dick and I were discussing what I should work on next. I wanted to try my hand at writing a romantic comedy."

Cal didn't laugh or say anything about romantic comedy. Instead he snored softly.

I'd gotten used to that as well this last year—his snoring, not his falling asleep mid-conversation.

I twirled the engagement ring on my finger.

It felt right.

I looked at the man sleeping on the couch next to me. He felt right.

He'd asked me to marry him on Christmas the year we met…in August. That was fast. I'd married fast once. And while I'd gotten three wonderful sons from that marriage, it hadn't lasted.

I'd been afraid to trust the feelings I had for Cal.

It was over a year since he'd asked, and this summer we'd celebrate knowing each other for two years. And I realized that it wasn't the amount of time that made me feel confident that saying yes to marrying Cal was the right thing to do ... it was Cal himself.

I loved him so much, and I felt confident he loved me, too.

He was taking time from work to help me figure out who killed Mellie.

For the first time, we were going to work together.

And that felt right, as well.

I leaned down and kissed his forehead. He woke up and pulled my kiss lower, to his lips. "Come to bed," he said, his voice all *Sam-Elliotty* with sleep. "We'll work on this after we've had some sleep."

I didn't argue.

I followed the man I loved—the man I was going to marry—to bed. I'd start interviewing people who were at the party myself after I got some sleep.

After-I-got-some-sleep was three hours later.

Jerome and Peri were still in bed. So was Cal.

I was wearing a pair of sweats, and a sweatshirt that Peri had made up for the cast of *Steamed*. It had a picture of Cilla in a French maid's outfit, her well-manicured fingers clutching a feather duster. The caption read, *Cleaning is Murder on a Manicure.*

I studied the three-page guest list. I knew my family and friends wouldn't kill a fly and had no motive for murdering Mellie. I started crossing them off.

When I was done I looked at the much shorter list. The people who were left were mainly the cast of the movie and the caterers from Honey's restaurant, *Psst*.

If you'd asked me before the Mortie Award Ceremony who I thought was capable of murder, I'd have said Mellie—hands down.

Without a doubt.

She was a megalomaniac. She hated that she was playing a secondary character. She really hated that Cilla had been cast to play me.

Basically, she didn't seem to like much...other than herself.

Unfortunately, Mellie couldn't be the murderer. And though I was pretty sure anyone else in the cast would have liked to have killed her more than once, I didn't honestly think they had. But while I took my family and friends off my suspect list, I didn't feel I knew the cast well enough to simply remove them.

I kept their names in my suspect column, but that gave me a much shorter list.

Detective Charlie's pool of suspects was going to be much larger than mine because he couldn't immediately eliminate my family and friends. I thought that might give me a better chance of catching the murderer.

Granted, my crossing people off my suspect list like that wasn't logical. But I wasn't a real detective. I never wanted to be a real detective. So I didn't care if my method was logical. I didn't care if it was procedure. I didn't even care if it made me ditzy. I just wanted to find out who killed Mellie. And I was sure that everyone I'd crossed off my list hadn't done it.

I sent Honey a text and asked for a list of everyone who'd catered the party.

But frankly, they weren't high on my suspect list. Why? Because they didn't know Mellie well enough to have a motive. I mean, I'd spent most of my adult life working in a service industry. I'm sorry to say there are a lot of people like Mellie, but most self-involved people didn't notice service people. We were invisible to them. It's hard to annoy someone so much they want to kill you if to you they're invisible.

I was leaning toward someone in the cast.

And that was awful because other than Mellie, I'd liked everyone in the cast.

I pulled up the movie credits on Net Movie Database and rolled the sweatshirt cuff around in my fingers as I stared at the cast list. Most everyone, while nice to me, hadn't come to my house. Cilla and Dylan had. Cilla spent a week trailing me after she'd signed on to play me in the movie. We'd become close.

Her husband, Dylan, was cast as Big G. Despite the fact they were actors, they hadn't put on airs. They seemed like a normal, happy couple. The kind of married couple Cal and I might hang out with once we were married. I reached for the ring on its chain and then realized it was on my finger now.

I'd start thinking about the wedding after I solved this case.

When I'd investigated Mr. Banning's case, I'd been anonymous. No one noticed another maid or caterer.

When I'd investigated the stolen paintings, I hadn't been exactly anonymous, but I'd had Dick as my sidekick, playing an insurance investigator.

And my Christmas mystery? I'd had access because everyone knew me.

Now, I was going to talk to people as myself... with Cal. There was no anonymity. Everyone knew me, and everyone

I was going to interview would know exactly why I was there. And someone I was going to talk to—someone I'd met, and potentially liked—was going to be the murderer. They'd have every reason to lie to me.

So maybe the trick was going to be talking to everyone, taking detailed notes and then figuring out whose story was different. I thought of all the cop shows I loved to watch. I thought about books from *Trixie Belden* to *Nancy Drew*.

In cop shows, suspects generally said too much. They didn't wait for a lawyer. Instead, they thought they could lie their way out of the charges.

Lies.

Lies always caught up with people. Liars goofed up and forgot part of their lie, or made the lie so elaborate it stuck out in the sea of generalities.

Cal came up behind me, leaned over the back of the chair and wrapped his arms around my shoulders. "I can hear you thinking," he murmured by my ear.

I turned and looked at my fiancé. "Are you really going to help me?"

He nodded, then leaned down and took my hand in his. "I love how this looks on your finger."

"I love how your hand looks on my hand."

Yeah, we were very, very sappy. Almost embarrassingly so. But I didn't plan on mentioning it to anyone. He sat down and we went all new-fiancé-mushy for a few more minutes.

Finally, demushed, Cal asked, "So what were you thinking about when I came in?"

"I was thinking that my advantage this time is I don't have to be a cop. I don't have go by the book...I don't even have to acknowledge that there's a book. I've completely eliminated most of Detective Charlie's suspect list. People

I'm absolutely positive aren't capable or have no motive to kill Mellie." I waited for him to tell me that's not how it was done.

"The cop part of me says that anyone is capable of murder, given the right circumstances. That's why when someone dies, we look to their spouse, or the people close to them for both the murderer and for the motive."

I started to protest, but Cal held up a hand. "If someone hurt your boys?"

I had to acknowledge he was right. "Fine. You've got a point, but—"

He interrupted. "Despite the fact I have a point, I'm with you. I think our friends and family can be moved off our suspect list, or at least moved way to the bottom. Mellie was an obnoxious woman. No one liked her. But not liking someone isn't enough of a motive for murder. I'm sure it wasn't your family or Tiny or Peri, Jerome...." He started naming all our friends and family and basically eliminated everyone I'd already eliminated.

The fact his list of non-suspects matched mine so perfectly made me all weak in the knees. "If we didn't have a murderer to find, I'd take you to bed right now and share my hidden stash of Poptarts with you."

"The boys moved out, so why do you hide them?"

I gave him a look, and he threw up his hands and shot me an award-winning innocent look. "Hey, I wouldn't stoop so low as to steal your Poptarts."

"Oh, yeah? Who got into the Pringles by lifting the paper seal, taking most of the stack, and then putting the paper and then plastic lid back in place? Like you said, the boys are in their college dorms, so they can be ruled out as suspects."

"I—" he started.

"When I went to get the Pringles the only thing left in the container was crumbs."

He laughed. "I have no idea what you're talking about."

I harrumphed him.

"Why don't we both take half of the didn't-do-it list and start making calls. Let's see what they remember. What they saw. General for most of the night, and as specifically as possible for the time between when Mellie arrived and when she died."

I nodded. "Okay."

We both went to work and only slowed down when Peri and Jerome came down and left to go out for dinner.

"We won't be home till late," Peri said. "I thought you and Cal would be busy with the case."

And we were.

As we worked our way through the lists, I learned something about investigations that I hadn't learned my first three times round…grunt work is boring.

I soon fell into a pattern of questions.

Did anything at the party stand out for you?

Did you see Mellie come into the party?

Did you see her talking to anyone?

Did you talk to her? If so, what did she say?

Did you see her go upstairs?

Did you see anyone else go upstairs?

Did you hear or see anything unusual?

I used a different variation of the first question at the end of the interview thinking that as they talked maybe it would remind them of something else…something that could be important.

The questions varied slightly and their order varied, but that was the gist of it.

I asked myself those same questions.

Did anything stand out for me?

Yes. The fact that so many friends and family showed up for me. My family and Lottie came all the way from Erie. The boys came from their college campuses.

Did I see Mellie come into the party?

No. The first time I noticed her she was talking to Jonas Miller. He'd played Cal in the movie. Sean, the director, was thrilled when Jonas signed on. Jonas had made quite a name for himself in blockbuster movies playing villains. This was a made for TV movie, not even a network movie, so having him in a lead role was huge. Don't get me wrong, I love The HeartMark Channel. But this wasn't a move up for Jonas. It wasn't even a lateral move. It was a move down.

I'd asked him why he took the role. He'd been sweet when he said, "It was a hell of a script, and this was the first time someone offered to let me play a hero. I'd like to know how that feels."

I liked Jonas. I didn't know him well enough to cross him off my suspect list, but I liked him enough to want it not to be him.

Did I see or hear anything unusual?

I'd seen Peri and she'd told me she asked Cal to ask Mellie to leave. I'd been pleased because I didn't want Mellie at the party—a party for my friends and family.

Cal had admitted he might have been one of the last people to see Mellie alive.

"How're the interviews, Quince?" he asked from the doorway.

"Do you think we can find another white-board? I want to put together as much of a timeline as I can. I thought about a spreadsheet, but I think a white-board timeline would be more effective."

"Sure. I'll go get it, then we'll enter info and brainstorm."

Cal ran to the store to buy another white-board and Dick dropped in.

My writing mentor had become a very good friend. He hugged me close. "Quincy, I'm so sorry something like this ruined your big night."

I hugged him back. "Thanks."

"I feel guilty," he said as he took a seat in my kitchen.

He looked guilty. As if the weight of the world was on his shoulders. "Why would you feel guilty, Dick?" I asked as I sat down next to him.

"Because I've had calls all day. No one wants to bother you, so they all went through me and Deanne. They want to know if you're looking into who killed Mellie. I told them all exactly where they could put that question. Mellie Adams was an awful woman. I only met her twice, but everyone in town knows how awful she was on set. But it seems macabre to be so excited about capitalizing on the woman's murder."

"I know. That's how I feel, too."

He reached across the counter and patted my hand. "Just walk away from this one, Quince. You're a talented writer, a great mom, and a wonderful business owner. You don't have to have amateur detective on your list of accomplishments. The other two times were flukes. And don't you worry. Deanne's telling everyone to leave you alone and not to hound you. And I'm … well, I wanted to stop in and see if you need anything."

I took his hand and led him into the living room. "Tell me what you remember."

He sighed. "You're not going to stop." It was a statement, not a question.

I shook my head.

He said, "Well, another reason it took me this long to come over is I was drunk last night. I fell asleep in on the couch in Jerome's study. I don't remember much after that, except...."

"Except?" I prompted.

"I'd gone to the bar but realized I couldn't handle another drink, so I went into the study to try and clear my head. The den was right next to where Peri had them set up the bar, so it was easy to get there and collapse. I had this really strange dream. Lady Gaga was dancing with Pink. Lady Gaga said, "*I know what you did. You can have anyone that you want, just not him. Leave him alone. I won't tell you again.*"

"Lady Gaga and Pink?" I laughed.

"Yes, then Pink said, *You're a fool* and stormed away." He paused a moment and said, "They both had very deep voices."

I laughed. "I'm glad you put that drink down."

"Me, too. I canceled my meeting and went home and crashed. My head's killing me now, and I can't imagine how I'd be feeling if I'd kept drinking."

"So do you remember anything else?"

Dick shook his head. "The next thing I remember is Cilla shaking me awake and telling me that the cops were there and no one had seen you or Cal. I was afraid..."

He hugged me. "I'm just glad you're okay. And I came here to tell you to stay out of this. I know, I was excited when you investigated the art heist, but Quincy, there's a murderer on the loose, and I don't want you messing with it."

"But Dick, how can I not? Everyone I love was at that party. That means, everyone I love is a suspect in the cops' eyes. Even you."

For a moment he was surprised, as if the thought he was a suspect hadn't occurred to him. Then he said in a very shaky voice, "You're my friend, Quincy. I don't want to have anything happen to you."

"And I don't want anything to happen to you or any of my other friends, so—"

"I'll tell Cal," he threatened. "If you won't listen to reason, I'll tell your future-fiancé and he'll…"

I waved my ring finger at him. "There's no almost anymore and you don't have to tell Cal—"

The door opened and Cal came in. I could see the giant white-board on the walkway. "Want to give me a hand."

"Wait, you're buying her a new white-board?" Dick asked.

"He's taking time off from work and helping me. The detective on the case knows I'm asking questions. It's all good," I told my friend. "Grab the door, will you?"

I went down and hefted the white-board with my fiancé, and we carried it into the living room and sat it by my original one.

"You two have been busy," Dick said as he wandered over to the board and studied it. He turned around and looked at Cal. "You keep her safe. She's an award-winning writer, with a wonderful career in front of her. She's also one of my dearest friends. Don't let whoever the murderer is get near her."

"I won't," Cal said solemnly.

I cleared my throat. "Let's not forget who saved who when I investigated Mr. Banning's murder."

They both ignored me, and Dick shook his head. "It's going to be hard work keeping her safe. She doesn't have any common sense."

"Tell me about it," Cal said. "Keeping my fiancée safe is going to be a full-time job, I suspect."

"I'm standing right here," I yelled, waving my hands. "And I have plenty of common sense."

They both laughed, and Cal casually wrapped his arm around me as the three of us studied the board.

❧ ❧ ❧

That night, Big G brought us pasta and a bottle of wine. He noticed my ring right off and hugged us both. Of course, when he hugged Cal, there was a lot of manly backslapping going on as well.

The three of us sat staring at the two white-boards that now occupied the wall of the house. "Where were you at the party when Mellie came in?" I asked him as I slurped some killer marinara.

Thinking the phrase *killer marinara* made me a bit queasy, and I set down my fork.

Big G didn't seem to notice. "I was talking to Honey when Mellie came in. She started to hum the theme of *Jaws*." He smiled, then he must realized he'd just told us that Honey didn't like Mellie and worried what we'd think because he said, "No, that's not what I meant I—"

I took his head. "G, it's okay. No one liked Mellie. Not liking someone doesn't mean you go out and murder them. I didn't like her, but I didn't kill her. And I certainly don't think Honey did. It's fine. Tell me what you remember. Maybe you saw something."

He shook his head. "I don't think so. Honey hummed *Jaws* and then noticed that the line for drinks was getting long, so she went to pitch in at the bar, and I went to help out, too."

"She was a guest, not hired to tend bar," I grumbled.

"She is a friend who wanted the party to be a success, so she helped out."

"Fine. Anything else?"

"I saw Cal talking to Mellie. She looked pissed—"

"That's her default expression," I grumbled.

"And then she stormed up the stairs. A while later, I saw Cal racing up the stairs."

"How long?"

"Four or five minutes? Maybe a little more. Maybe a lot longer. The whole night is a blur. Honey and I finished working at the bar and were on our way out back again to look for you. The next thing I know, there were cops and people running upstairs. No one would tell us what was going on. I couldn't find you or Cal. I. ...."

He let the sentence fade and looked as if he were trying to collect himself. "You scared the hell out of me. I was worried that something had happened to one or both of you."

"Why would you think that?" Cal asked.

"Cal, remember the first time you brought Quincy into the restaurant? I said if you locked her up I'd break her out of jail?"

"I think you said you'd slip me a file," I said, smiling. I liked Big G from the moment I met him. And it wasn't just that he was a heck of a cook and fed me.

He laughed. "Same difference. Either way, you've had a few…uh…incidents. When I saw the cops, I was afraid that you'd had another and there was more than a threat of jail. No one had seen either of you for a while."

I patted his hand. Cal's best friend was a nice man. Over the almost two years I'd known him, he'd become my friend, too.

As if our conversation had become too emotional for him, Big G said, "And how can I woo you away from Cal if one or both of you is in jail, or worse?"

I waved my engagement ring at him to remind him, and he raised an eyebrow. "Well, until you guys say I-do, I still have a chance."

I laughed and Cal mock-scowled as he asked, "I-do's are as good as said as far as you're concerned, buddy. Can you think of anything else? Anyone at the party seem less than happy?"

"Your doppelganger," he nodded at me, "and the guy that played me had words."

"Cilla and Dylan?"

"I just know them as Quincy2 and Me2."

"They're married," Cal said.

"Look at you," I teased my fiancé. "You're almost ready to write for the tabloids if you decide on a career change."

He snorted. "Not likely." Then turned to Big G and said, "So the married couple...?"

"Let's just say that they had a married fight of some kind."

I'd seen Dylan and Cilla together throughout the filming and I'd never seen them as anything but a lovely couple. They were the kind of couple who still holds hands. The kind of acting couple who run lines together.

"No one else mentioned that to me, how about you, Cal?"

"No one else said anything to me, either."

"They were outside, sitting on that bench in the middle of all those bushes. You know the one with the sandbox next to it."

"That's not a sandbox, it's a serenity garden," I said. Peri had tried to convince Jerome he needed to meditate. He insisted he wasn't the kind of man who sat around and said *Namaste* and *ohm*. So, she tried the serenity garden. He'd scoffed at the idea that raking sand might relax him, but she'd confided that she'd caught him at it more than once.

"That's not a garden," Big G argued, "its a sandbox."

I decided not to argue the point. That area he was talking about was tucked away and designed to be private. "You're sure they were arguing?"

"I work in a restaurant. I know what a couple who's fighting looks like. Especially a couple in public who's trying to keep the fight private."

I'd been afraid all I was going to be able to do was make calls and put together a timeline. But now, I had something. I looked at Cal … *we* had something. A direction to start looking.

"What do you say we go see Cilla and Dylan tomorrow?" I asked my fiancé.

"Sounds like a plan."

CHAPTER FIVE

THE NEXT MORNING, I was in the kitchen reading *GoErie.com*, my hometown's online version of the newspaper. I love to keep up on what's happening in good old Erie, Pennsylvania. But today's article me made me feel uncomfortable.

The paper had written articles about me in the past, and local television news stations had done reports. They'd all covered me when I'd solved Mr. Banning's murder and then solved the painting heists. They'd even told good old Sherlock Holmes to move over. They wrote about my movie deal, and then they sent a very nice reporter with a passion for plaid out to follow me when the movie was in production.

Here's the thing, I am not logic minded like Sherlock. I'm absolutely in love with the new BBC incarnation of the character—it doesn't hurt that I love Martin Freeman and Benedict Cumberbatch. And I love the new US television version, *Elementary*. But I could never work all logical and deductiony.

Let's not forget that a lot of movie reviewers referred to my character in the movie as ditzy. More than that, they said the only reason I'd solved either case was clearly just dumb luck. One reviewer went so far as to mention that if Lucille Ball were still acting, they'd have had her play me rather than Cilla.

Cilla laughed off the review.

If you asked me what my investigative procedure looked like, I wouldn't have said logical or comical. And I certainly wouldn't have said ditzy.

I'd have said, I investigated like a mom and business owner

When the boys were little, I'd take a laundry basket through the house and pick up all the minutia three boys generated. Dirty socks, wads of paper, candy wrappers, video games, books. . . .

That's what I tried to do with my 'investigations.' I gathered up information. Minutia really. That was the mom part.

The business owner part had to do with some of that, with a bit of my gut mixed in. When Mac'Cleaners got calls from new clients, I had to talk to them and get a feel for what they really wanted. Most would say they wanted their house cleaned.

But for some that meant the basics . . . Pine Sol, a dustcloth, and the Dyson.

For others, it meant moving every piece of furniture, as well as cleaning all the curtains. It meant baseboards and ceiling fans. When I interviewed new clients, my job was to listen, take in everything they said, and then figure out what they really meant. I had to dig through everything and pull out what really mattered.

That's what we were going to do today. I had my figurative clothesbasket all ready to visit with Dylan and Cilla. I'd just go out and collect minutia until I stumbled on some clue that would lead us to the killer.

I turned off my iPad and took a long drink of my tepid coffee as Cal walked into the kitchen.

"Good morning, fiancée," he said with far more chipperness than seven a.m. called for. Cal was not a chipper seven a.m. guy by nature. But there he was, grinning at me … chipperness personified.

He leaned down, kissed my forehead, and headed over to the coffeemaker. "It feels weird to not set an alarm. I thought I'd sleep in until nine or later, and yet, here I am."

"I get that. When Theresa started taking a more active role in the office at the business, I thought I'd do some major sleeping in. Turns out that between kids and work, I was broken. I couldn't sleep late any more. I didn't set an alarm and yet I was up early every day. Turns out, mornings are my best writing time."

"You're not writing today." He brought his coffee over and sat down next to me.

This was how I pictured our life together. Me and Cal, sipping coffee together in the morning. Him going to work, me staying home and writing. Talking about our days over dinner. Just being together.

Today we had more to do than linger over coffee. "I don't think I'll be doing much writing for the time being. You and I have to catch a killer."

"Were you working on the case? You could have woken me."

I shook my head. "No, I was reading the Erie Times-News."

"You don't look pleased."

"I was the subject of a front page article. Local girl goes to Hollywood, fails at acting, starts a successful cleaning business, then starts a potential successful screenwriting career—"

"I'd say your Mortie proved that you're not potentially successful, you are."

"*Steamed* could be a fluke. Plus, I don't actually have my Mortie. It's at the murder scene."

"But you won one, and that's proof enough," he said with fiancé pride.

"Thanks. You know, the Morties are a rather new award…and they've been involved with two murders. Do you think there might be some curse involved with winning a Mortie?" Frankly, winning hadn't done Mr. Banning much good, and right now, it wasn't looking so good for me either. Not that I was a suspect, but because someone I know wasn't just a suspect but a murderer.

"No. Mr. Banning won one and was killed with it, but you won yours and someone else got killed…and not with yours."

"With someone else's," I said. Having two people murdered by a Mortie didn't seem to bode well for the awards.

"She didn't look bludgeoned to me. I purposefully didn't go in and study the body, but if the Mortie had killed her, I'd think she'd been…messier. I'll call Randolph and see if he's got anything preliminary from the ME."

"Tell Charlie I said hi when you call."

"You know, he might prefer you call him Detective, or even Detective Randolph." He paused a moment, then we both laughed.

"Yeah, he might prefer it, but we both know that's not going to happen. I think one of my jobs in this lifetime is to keep cops humble."

Cal snorted. "Back to the newspaper. What did they write that you didn't like?"

"No. The article was fine. Very nice, as a matter of fact. It's just that I've discovered I'm not a fan of the spotlight. And I guess that makes the fact I came out here to be an actress seem funny."

"Well, you figured out that maybe you should be writing movies, not acting in them, that's what matters."

I shook my head. "It took me forty years to find out what I wanted to be when I grew up. You've always known who you were."

He laughed as he took another sip of coffee. "No. I didn't intend to be a detective, much less a cop."

After almost two years, I was still occasionally surprised about some new Cal tidbit. "Really? What did you want to be?"

"When I was younger, I wanted to be a cowboy, but when I got older, I wanted to be a rodeo cowboy. I learned to rope."

"Really? Like with a lasso and the whole thing?"

He nodded.

"Did you have the hat, the boots, and the chaps?" I asked, as a delightful fantasy began playing in my head. One in which Cal wore the hat, the boots, and the chaps...and nothing else.

He chuckled and laughed. "Yes."

I told him about my fantasy.

Coffee, newspaper articles, and even the investigation were forgotten as I went into great, lurid detail about that new fantasy.

Two hours later, shortly after nine, we drove to Dylan and Cilla's.

We'd talked about calling first, but Cal said as a detective he'd always found there was something to be said about the element of surprise.

Since I didn't have anonymity on my side this time, surprise was going to have to do.

Dylan and Cilla lived in a modest house in Palisades. Well, modest in any other market. I come from Erie. When I first saw how much houses cost in LA I was in shock. For what a paid for my more-modest-than-Dylan-and-Cilla's house in LA, I could have bought a huge house on the bay in Erie.

"Do you have a script?" Cal asked as I parked.

"A script?"

He shot me a devilish look that made my knees go weak. "I thought I'd try Hollywood jargon. Do you know what you're going to ask them?"

"No, I've never known the specifics of what I'm going to ask before I ask someone. I'll start with the basics, I guess. The things I've already asked almost everyone on the phone. I'll ask them what they remember about the party, and specifically about Mellie's entrance, and of course about their fight."

"All right."

"We're not grilling suspects," I reminded my coppish fiancé. "I'm talking to friends."

"You're talking to friends who *are* suspects until they're not," he insisted.

I shook my head. "By that logic you're a suspect."

"I guess I am."

"No, you're not. You couldn't murder someone."

He grabbed me by the shoulders and spun me around to face him. "Listen, Quince, I need to be clear about this. Everyone has it in them. Even the most mild-mannered person can be pushed too far. They can take a life. Sometimes it's self-defense. Sometimes self-preservation. Sometimes anger. Fear. I've arrested mild-mannered accountants, stay-at-home moms, and college professors. I've arrested career criminals and one-time-offenders."

"But not—"

"Tell me, if someone was threatening your boys, would you do anything it took to save them?"

I knew instantly that he was right. I'd do whatever it took to save my sons if I needed to.

I looked at Mr. Tough Detective and knew that the same applied to him. I'd do whatever it took to save him. I didn't say the words. I could see that he knew what I was thinking.

"I know you've trusted your gut in the Banning and painting investigations. While your gut might be a good starting point, in this case, you know pretty much everyone at the party. The only person you didn't like is the person who's dead. There's a good chance that whoever killed her is someone you know and like. Your gut might not be trustworthy. You need to understand that."

The fact that he was right made my heart ache but I nodded. "I'll try and remember that."

"Remember this, too. ... The person who killed Mellie will not be happy that you're talking to people. And once someone's killed once, it's easier to do it again. There's a chance that they'll kill again and I don't want them coming after you."

"I'll be careful."

He kissed me. "Good. And if you forget, I'll be here keeping an eye on you."

We walked, hand in hand like two heartsick high school students and knocked on the door.

Cilla answered.

Cilla was the type of woman who looked good first thing in the morning. Even worse, she looked good first thing in the morning when she'd obviously been working out. She was wearing yoga pants, a sports bra covered by a hardly there shirt and a towel around her neck. The towel was the most generous part of her ensemble.

I sucked in my stomach, which after three kids had a tendency to pooch.

Cilla took the towel from around her neck and patted off her face. "Quincy, Cal, what a pleasant surprise. Come on in. I was just finishing my workout. Dylan was making the smoothies. I'll have him make you two one if you want to try?" She led us toward the back of the house. "It's his secret recipe. Fresh fruit, kale and ..."

Two glasses of very green smoothies were on the counter, and Dylan was smiling as we entered the kitchen.

"...avocado." Cilla finished. "Look who the cat dragged in."

"No thanks on the smoothies," I said. The concoctions looked suspiciously...green. For years I avoided split pea soup because of its greenness. When I finally tried it, I realized I'd been missing out. But just because one green thing was good, didn't mean all green things were. Look at Brussels sprouts. Those were green...and not good at all.

Cal's expression said he agreed with me and I added, "We already had breakfast."

"So what brings you to our humble abode?" Dylan asked as he picked up a glass and took a slurp.

"We'd like you to run through the party again. See if you remembered anything else that could be helpful."

They carried their green smoothies to the table and nodded for us to take a seat.

"I've done nothing but think about the events at the party," Cilla said. "I tried to think things through, like you did in *Steamed*. But Quincy, I didn't see anything more than I've already told you. Mellie came in. She tried to kick up a fuss. Cal asked her to leave. And the next thing I knew, cops were coming into the house and she was dead."

"Same here," Dylan said. "I didn't see or hear anything."

"What did you two fight about?" I asked bluntly, without preamble.

That surprised them. You could see it on their faces. They didn't think anyone knew. "Out by the meditation garden," I added.

"Meditation garden?" Dylan asked.

"Sandbox," Cal clarified.

"Oh."

Dylan looked at Cilla, who looked at him. They had a silent conversation.

I know, that sounds like an oxymoron, *a silent conversation*, but I was well acquainted with them. My parents used to have them when we were growing up. My brothers and I would see them look at each other and come to a decision about this or that, without ever having said a word.

I'd seen Tiny and Sal have them as well.

Maybe not everyone in the world had them, but I'd always known that couples who were really in sync could have them. Cal and I had just silently conversed about smoothies.

Dylan and Cilla were really in sync.

They broke eye contact and Cilla looked at me, as Dylan nodded.

"I got offered a role in another movie," Cilla said. "A starring role."

"That's wonderful?" I half said, half asked.

"You'd think that it was." Cilla nodded toward Dylan. "Especially when Dylan got offered the male lead."

"Hey, congrats, Dylan." Again, it was a halfhearted offering because I could sense that something wasn't right. There was no excitement in her voice.

"That seems like something to celebrate, not something to fight about," Cal threw in.

"We were planning on taking some time off and trying to have a baby. I want to put it off until after this," Cilla said.

Dylan looked annoyed. "And I pointed out that putting it off isn't a viable option for much longer."

"He's saying that I'm getting old."

If Cilla was old then I was decrepit.

As a woman, I knew that Dylan's words were fighting words, and from his expression, so did he.

"Well, I. ..." I let the sentence trail off because frankly, I didn't have a clue what to say to that.

Rather than looking mad, they both laughed. Cilla said, "We've decided that we're not going to try, and we're not going to not-try. We're going to see what happens and make the movie."

"And we're going to look into adoption," Dylan added. "There are so many kids out there who need a home, and we have a home."

I'd liked Dylan and Cilla from the start. I was pretty sure I liked them even more now. "There's a couple from my hometown who couldn't have kids and so they adopted a bunch. The paper ran a couple articles about them."

Cilla nodded. "We've talked about it and we're going to see what happens on the baby front, but pregnancy or not, we're pretty sure that we're going to adopt."

"Well, congratulations on the movie and the family," I said.

"If someone saw us fighting, do you think that will make the cops think we did it?" Cilla looked a little nervous. "Not that we did anything, but I don't think being a focus of a police investigation is something I'd relish. I know some people in Hollywood live by the adage that all press is good press... I'm not one of them."

Now, if I were writing this as a script, a couple might be fighting because the wife found out that Mellie had an affair with the husband. Or the husband found out Mellie had an affair with the wife.

But neither of them could stand Mellie any more than I could, so I couldn't imagine either of them having an affair, which would lead to romantic jealousy being an issue.

And both of them had bigger roles in the movie, so career jealousy wasn't it.

Of course, Mellie might have been the one who was jealous and started trouble...trouble that ended up with her dead. But looking at Dylan and Cilla holding hands and talking about starting a family one way or another, I knew it wasn't them.

I knew it in my gut.

I remembered Cal's words of warning, but they didn't matter.

Cilla and Dylan didn't do it. But maybe they saw something.

"Could you run through everything you remember one more time?" I asked, and as they nodded, I said, "Do you mind if I record it?"

They didn't mind, and they also didn't offer anything new. They'd seen most of the cast at one point or another. They'd spent a lot of time with Jonas and Shia—aka Cal and Tiny in the movie. "I think they're a couple," Cilla stage-whispered.

Dylan snorted. "I think that Shia wants them to be a couple. She's so excited to be doing real acting instead of her reality fodder, she's jumping from actor to actor, hoping one sticks and lends her acting some legitimacy."

I knew just what they were talking about, because I'd noticed it, too. At one time or another, Shia had been linked to almost every available man on set.

"But they didn't do it," Dylan said. "They were talking to us when the cops arrive."

"I didn't see anyone upstairs except you and Cal and the cops," Cilla said. "And of course we know that you and Cal didn't do it."

Well, I knew that, and I knew that Cal knew that, but if Detective Charlie was doing the same interviews I was—and I was sure that he was—would he know that?

❦ ❦ ❦

"Well, I don't think we're any further along than when we started," I told Cal as we drove away. "We didn't find out anything new."

"We found out Dylan and Cilla are going to start a family. What about you?" he asked.

"Huh?" I had kids so I was used to conversations that took sharp turns, but I wasn't sure where this one was turning to.

"After we're married, where do we stand on adding to the family?" Cal asked. "I know you have the boys."

Adding to the family?

That meant babies.

That meant nursing, late nights, and being puked on … or worse.

No, wait, it meant pregnancy first. Swollen ankles, puking for months.

My boys were all out of the house now and when Cal asked me to marry him, I'd put it on hold for a year because I wanted to try being on my own … well, on my own with him by my side.

What I'd decided is on-my-own wasn't all its cracked up to be.

I missed having the boys under foot.

I even missed coming home and finding their mess and noise.

"Cal, I'm forty. I don't know if I could get pregnant. My eggs are old. Frankly, there's a good chance my eggs are fried."

"Getting pregnant isn't the only way to have a child, Quince. Dylan and Cilla said as much. There are kids out there who are looking for a home. More than that, for a family. Maybe we're who they've been looking for?"

"You'd be willing to do that?" To have a kid and not have swollen ankles … that didn't sound like such a bad deal to me.

"Listen, I've been around for almost two years, and I love your boys. They're not my blood, I wasn't around when they were little, but that doesn't mean I don't think of them as family. When I said I was sure you could kill someone to save them, I knew that because I could, too."

Now, maybe talking about murder like that didn't sound sweet, but in this context, it was.

"Frankly," he continued, "one of the things I love about you is how you and Jerome have always put the boys first. You might not be married anymore, but you've parented together. And I really love that you have never looked at Peri as a threat, but as one more person to love your boys. How could I not have realized that blood doesn't make a parent, or a family?"

I felt myself tear up and I didn't know what to say. But I should have known that I didn't need to say anything. Cal understood because Cal always understood me.

He reached over and patted my hand. "Just think about what you want and we'll talk about it. As for me, I don't need to procreate, and I could spend the rest of my life with just you, me, our friends and families. But I think there's a chance there's a child out there waiting for us to find them."

"Right now I think the only finding we have to do is find the murderer, and then we'll talk weddings and adding to the family."

He reached over again, took my hand in his and gave it a squeeze. "True that."

"Please, never, never say that again."

He laughed. I laughed. And I realized I didn't feel any stress in coming to a decision because I knew that whatever I decided, Cal would be okay with it.

I squeezed his hand back.

I was a lucky woman, despite the fact I'd found my second dead body.

CHAPTER SIX

ABOUT A HALF HOUR after we got home, my cellphone rang and I knew I couldn't put off this particular call another minute.

"Hi, Mom," I said with as much chipperness as I could muster.

"Quincy, how could you let us get on a plane when you'd found another dead body?" my mother asked loudly over the phone. And since Judith Quincy Mac was a *Lady* with a capital *L*, she wasn't prone to speaking loudly.

Firmly. Decisively. Yes.

But not loudly and certainly not shrilly.

I'd never tell her, but there was a chance that in addition to loud she was just a bit shrill at the moment.

"Mom, things happened so fast, and by the time I could call you the plane was on its way back to Erie."

"And when you did call, you left a message, and you haven't answered my calls since."

"I did, too."

"Saying, *Mom, I can't talk now, I'll call when I can. Just talk to the cops when they call you*, doesn't count."

Yes, I'd been putting off this call, I'll admit it. To myself. Maybe even to Cal. But I wasn't about to tell my mother that.

Here's the thing, I loved my mom and she loved me. And I suspected there was a chance she'd offer to come out and help. And I didn't want her anywhere near some crazy murderer.

As if on cue, she said, "I would have helped you find out who murdered Mellie. Although, having met Mellie, I'm not shocked someone finally lost it with her. She made a pass at your father. Did I tell you that? Her and that Shia-person who played Tiny. They both made passes at him. Although, when that Shia-person found out he was *only a doctor*—that's what she said, *only a doctor*—she unpassed. Mellie didn't care if he was a doctor or not. And she also didn't care if he was married or not." She sniffed, then added, "I don't know how you work with people like that."

"I don't. Not really. I mainly work by myself or with Dick."

I knew my mother loved Dick. Not in a way that was threatening to my father, but in a way that was just a bit of a girl-crush. Mom and Dick were best buddies.

"Now, Dick is a true gentleman," she said. "So tell me what's going on?"

"I don't have much to report." Frankly, I didn't have anything to report.

"Did you set up your white-board?" Mom asked.

"Yes," I admitted. "And Cal took some time off to help me look into this. The detective on the case, Detective Charles Randolph, isn't threatening to arrest me. He said to come to him if I found something, but I haven't found anything."

"Quincy, I—"

I didn't want Mom offering to come out and help find a murderer, because I didn't want her anywhere near whoever killed Mellie. So I decided to sidetrack her in the most efficient way I possibly could. "And, Mom, it's official. I'm engaged."

"What?"

Wow, Judith Quincy Mac was loud twice in one conversation. That was some kind of record.

So I told her what happened.

"Congratulations, honey. Tell Cal for me, too. When will you be coming home?"

I was going to say I didn't know, but then she finished her sentence. "We've got a wedding to plan."

"I thought Cal and I would just do something small here and I—"

"Quincy you eloped with Jerome and I didn't say anything, but you and Cal? I want a wedding. I deserve a wedding. I was mother of the groom when your brothers got married, and though the ceremonies were lovely, your sisters-in-law and their mothers did the heavy planning. I want to plan."

"But Mom, I really don't want—"

"That's fine. You don't worry about a thing. I'll call Tiny. I'm sure she'll agree to help me put this together. And Peri. She'll help, too."

Peri was one thing, but Tiny? "Oh, Mom, don't call Tiny. Please. She'll help you plan it all right. I can't do it again. I've barely recovered from her planning her own wedding. Please don't let her fill her office with magazines, swatches, and samples. I beg you." Really, that sounded pathetic, but I'd only just survived Tiny's wedding. And she was a good friend. She'd go even more overboard on mine.

"I've talked to your detective, but I need to hear from you. And congratulations again. I'll give Tiny a call as well."

"Mom—"

"As for the case, call Dick. Between you, Dick, and Cal you'll find the murderer before I come back to LA to meet with you, Tiny, and Peri about the wedding."

I'm pretty sure she put more faith in Dick than in me and Cal. Despite the wedding-threat, I smiled. Then I had an image of Tiny's pre-wedding office and tried again. "Mom, you're a doctor. You can't just leave your practice to plan a wedding."

"Watch me."

I hung up and groaned.

"What's wrong?" Cal asked.

"I told my mom we're officially engaged."

"And she wasn't happy?" He looked concerned.

I shook my head. "No. Saying she was happy would be like saying the ocean's kind of big. She's over the moon, Cal. And she's coming back to California soon to help plan the wedding." I hummed the theme of *Jaws*.

Cal obviously realized this might not be a good thing because he said, "You did tell her we want to keep it small?"

"Oh, I did," I assured him. "She's cutting me out of the planning and going directly to Tiny and Peri."

"Oh, no," Cal said. He'd listened to my Tiny wedding woes more than once.

"You can say that again."

I stared at the white-board, but visions of orange brides-maid dresses and doves kept intruding.

I walked over and started crossing off more images.

I crossed off Dylan and Cilla. I crossed off Shia and Jonas. Though I knew I wanted to talk to them both, they'd been alibied.

I'd already crossed off Peri and Jerome. Not only did I know they didn't do it, but they'd been playing hosts.

Cal handed me a cup of coffee.

"You okay?"

"Sure. I mean, a dead actress was found in my son's bed. My friends and family are all on the suspect list. And my mom is going to enlist Tiny and Peri to plan my wedding. And truth is, I'm a fraud. I've solved thr—" I cut myself off.

I hadn't even told Cal about my Christmas mystery. "Two mysteries by total luck. I don't have a clue who to look at and what to do."

"I don't want to add to your annoyance, but...." He slid the local paper at me.

LA's Maid for Murder Does It Again
Local business owner, turned screenwriter, and Mortie winner, Quincy Mac, had her evening of celebration interrupted by another dead body...

Oh, come on. I'd accepted the fact that the Erie media was going to cover the murder, but LA is a huge market. There had to be bigger stories.

But there it was in black and white.

Well, boogers.

"So we'll keep going," Cal said when I'd finished reading the name-dropping article.

"Keep going?" I had no clue where to look next. How could you keep going if you didn't have a direction to go in?

"Yes. That's what you did before. You simply kept talking to people and taking notes, and eventually—"

I thought about my laundry basket analogy. I was afraid I could keep collecting facts from now till I was old and gray, and I'd never find the killer. "I lucked into the right answer."

"You know what Dick says about luck?" Cal asked with a grin that said he knew exactly what Dick said.

Dick was always spouting *helpful* sayings when I got stuck on a writing project.

"*Luck means being in the right place at the right time. So you've got to keep moving forward and looking for that place.*" I sighed. "I don't think it's one of his better sayings."

"But he's got a point. That's what I do when I work on a case. I keep looking at people until something comes up that makes me take a second look. We need to keep crossing people off our suspect list and when we get the potential murderer pool down enough, something will come up. I don't think it's really luck. It's more perseverance. That's how you solved your other two cases, and that's how we'll solve this. Now, we've had Cilla and Dylan alibi Shia and Jonas. That's four more people we've eliminated. Let's check with Shia and Jonas. We'll make sure their stories mesh with Cilla and Dylan's, and see if maybe they saw something different."

He sounded far more optimistic than I felt. To be honest, sometimes when you gathered up minutia in a laundry basket you just ended up with a bunch of dirty clothes. "Fine."

Cal kissed me. It was simply a non-thinking sort of kiss. An everyday sort of thing. And maybe that's what made it so sweet. Kissing me was just second nature to him now.

I turned and kissed him back in a much more thinking-about-it, but equally second nature sort of way. He didn't seem to mind.

When I pulled back he said, "Quince, I know it's not very glamorous, but that's the real truth about cop work. It's *not* glamorous. We don't solve cases in an hour show like *The Closer, Major Crimes,* or *Law and Order.*"

"I wish Mary McDonnell were in charge of this case." Sharon Raydor would have her crack team from *Major Crimes* on it, and they'd not only solved the crime, but coerced a plea deal from the murderer.

"Even she couldn't solve this in an hour. And I don't think any departments have a *CSI* quality crime lab that finds forensic evidence and makes the arrests themselves like the show does in under an hour. Police work is mainly nose to the grindstone, slogging through enough facts until you figure it out. Forensics gets a lot of the glory, and maybe our team will find something, but in most cases its just nose—"

"—to the grindstone and dumb luck," I finished.

"Nothing dumb about putting yourself in the right place at the right time."

"So we start. ..."

"We start crossing names off the list, one by one."

I nodded. "Let's start with Shia and then Jonas."

Cal nodded. "Sounds like as good a place as any."

Shiantay Miller was known as Shia to her coworkers and the millions of viewers of the hit reality series, *LA Shore* and *Casting Callers*. She was driven, beautiful and while not the most talented actress ever, she was competent.

Her birth name was Sheila Dubrinski.

We went to the address that the studio had given us. It was a middle class ranch that sat on a small incline only a few blocks from my house.

A giant, burly man who looked vaguely familiar opened the door. That was the thing about Hollywood. So many people worked as supporting cast on shows, that there was an overabundance of the population who looked vaguely familiar.

"Yeah?" the guy said, in a not overly friendly way.

"Hi, I'm Quincy Mac and I'm looking for Shia?"

"I know who you are. Shia doesn't live here." The man's tone was less than cordial. To be honest, it was rather hostile.

Cal slipped into super-cop mode at the sound. His body went ramrod straight, his expression was serious and gave nothing away, while his tone was all business. "This is the address the studio gave us."

"She lives in the apartment." He jerked a finger at the garage. A set of stairs climbed to a second story. "She's been so busy with acting gigs she hasn't had time to find a place of her own," he defended, though neither of us had said anything about the fact she lived over a garage.

"You're her landlord?" Cal asked.

"Her father," Mr. Grumpy Pants said.

"Oh, it's nice to meet Shia's father," I said and shook his hand. At first he seemed unwilling, but then he returned my greeting. "She was such a joy to work with. I can only imagine how proud you are."

Finally, he gave me a brief smile. "I am."

Cal nodded. "Have we met? You look familiar."

Shia's father paused, and when he spoke the animosity was gone. "I don't think so. I stopped in at the party after the Mortie's. Sheila invited me," he added quickly, as if he was afraid we might think he crashed.

"That must be it," Cal said. "If you were there, would mind telling us what if anything you saw?"

"You mean the murder?"

"Yes," I said. "That's what we came to see Shia about. We're trying to collect everyone's memories of the party, while they're still fresh."

He opened the door and let us in the house proper. "Can I get you all anything to drink?"

"No, we're fine. Do you mind if I record you? My note taking sucks."

"Fine." He offered us seats in the living room. It was spartan. There were no knick-knacks, so muss. There was functional furniture, and one painting of Shia over the fireplace.

"There's really not much to tell," he started. "I came to the party because Sheila—Shia," he corrected himself,

HOLLY JACOBS

"Invited me. It's been me and her since her mom ran out when she was five. Anyway, I found her. Had a quick drink with her. I was there when you made your speech. I loved the glasses, by the way."

I smiled. "I loved them, too. They're a tangible reminder that someone has always believed in me. That's a true gift."

"It is. I always believed in Sheila. I try to be her biggest supporter. She wants to be an actress—a real actress—and this movie was a step in the right direction. It's better than those reality shows she was in. They made her look—" He cut himself off.

He didn't need to go on. I knew just what he meant. *LA Shore* and *Casting Callers* both cast Shia as the wild child. That had to have been hard on her father to watch.

"It's all in how they cut the footage," he said. "She's not like that in real life."

And that was a father's blindness. Shia was exactly like the shows indicated. She was sweet, ambitious, and willing to use all her assets to get what she wanted.

Mellie was ambitious and willing to use her assets, too. But no one ever called her sweet.

Shia was. Getting angry with her would be like getting angry at a puppy who wanted your attention.

"*Steamed* was just the first movie in her career. She's going to have everything she's always wanted," he said.

I felt a kinship with Shia's father because I understood that. I wanted nothing less for Miles, Hunter, and Eli.

"Did you see anyone else? Talk to anyone else?"

He shook his head. "I was uncomfortable, to be honest. I'm not much for small talk. So, I stopped in and told Shia I was proud of her. Had a drink. Watched your speech and left. Sorry."

70

"Thanks. Every little bit helps. Someone's going to see something that helps."

"Someone always does," Cal said.

"We'll go talk to Shia now. But if you think of anything else, here's my card." I handed him a Mac'Cleaner's card.

"You still use your maid cards?" he asked with a smile.

I grinned. "I might write now," I always shied away from calling myself a writer ... it felt pretentious. "But I'm proud of my business and my job."

We left the house and walked across the driveway to the stairway on the outside of the garage and knocked on the door.

Shia, aka Shiantay, aka Shelia, answered the door. She was wearing a negligee. And that was a generous description. Really, it was a piece of silk the size of a hanky that was strategically place in order to cover up her girl bits. And by cover I mean, barely.

"Quincy," she said with a squeal, a small hop, and then she hugged me. I was terrified that the silk had slipped and was no longer strategically covering anything.

"And Officer Yummy." She went to hug him, but he took a step back on the tiny landing and placed himself behind me. Shia pouted.

"Come in," she said. "Can I get you something to drink? I've got some very nice wine and—"

"Shia, it's way too early to be drinking," I said.

"We didn't come for drinks. We came to talk to you about Quincy's party." Cal's voice was all coppish and businessy. I hadn't heard this particular tone since we first met.

We were standing in the middle of an open concept room. The kitchen was at one end, a living/dining area in the middle where we were standing, then a couple doors, which I'd guess led to a bedroom and a bathroom. It looked like someone threw up that pink stomach medicine on everything. Pink walls. Pink ceilings. A pink fuzzy sofa. Seriously. It looked like something a *Barbie* dream house might have used for an interior.

I tried to ignore the fact we were drowning in pink and living in fear that Shia's outfit was going to slip and simply concentrate on the task at hand. "Do you have a moment to go over what happened that night with us?" I managed.

"What do you mean, what happened?"

"We'd like you to go over everything you remember from that night," Cal, the detective, said.

"Please, have a seat," she said. She grabbed a robe from the back of the couch and slipped it on before sitting down. It wasn't much, but it was better.

"Do you mind if I tape this?" I was already pulling out my tape recorder and setting it down on the coffee table.

"Sure. I don't really have much to say. Let's see, we went to the award show, me and Jonas. Women everywhere want him, you know. He plays such a tough guy in most of his movies. A bad guy most of the time. His fans were so jealous I was his date."

It was obvious the fact other women were jealous was not a problem for Shia.

"I'm used to women being jealous of me. And I'm not talking about when I started my *meteoritic*," she said the word with long drawn-out emphasis, "career with *LA Shore*. It's been like that my whole life. I just talk to a boy, and rumors would fly and girlfriends would get mad." She sighed, as if that were truly a trial, but even though she tried to disguise it, her expression said she enjoyed the attention.

"My date Jonas and I went to all the big parties. And even though I was done in, we came to your party. Jonas insisted.

He said he owed you 'cause you stuck up for him getting the part of Cal. He went on and on about being typecast as a bad guy. You gave him the opportunity to play a tough cop, who was a sweet guy. A good guy. The hero."

Jonas was sweet and added that nuance to his performance as Cal.

"So we came to your party," Shia said. "Jonas was talking to people, so I made the rounds and talked to people, too. I spent an hour talking to this one guy and I knew he wasn't an actor. I thought he had to be a director or producer or something. I mean, he was kind of short, and not a looker, if you know what I mean. Turns out he was a lawyer. A married lawyer, no less."

I thought there was a good chance she was talking about Sal. He was the only married lawyer I could think of who would have been there. Her *not-a-looker* remark set my teeth on edge.

"But he was a nice guy, so I didn't really mind," she added, and I remembered why I liked Shia more than Mellie, though they both were looking to climb the ladder. Mellie would have made it clear to Sal that she minded he couldn't further her career. Shia never would.

"His wife called him and after that I found Jonas again. We were talking to Cilla and Dylan when my dad came in had a drink, then left. And then the cops were there saying Mellie was dead. And you and Cal were upstairs and we thought you might come down in handcuffs, but you didn't, probably 'cause he's a cop." She nodded in Cal's direction.

"Or maybe because the cops knew we didn't do anything," I pointed out.

She laughed. "Of course you didn't. Now, Mellie, she might have done someone in for walking on her lines or just annoying her. But you're nice Quincy, and he's," she pointed at Cal, "hunky, even if he's a cop."

Being annoyed at Shia would be like being annoyed by fireflies. "Anything else?"

"Nope."

"Did you see Mellie at all?" I asked.

"I think I saw her come in, but I didn't talk to her. She didn't like me, which was okay 'cause I didn't like her. She was jealous that Jonas took me to the awards. She thought every man on the set was in love with her."

I didn't mention that Shia seemed to feel the same way, instead I simply said, "Well, if you think of anything else will you give me a call?"

"Sure, I will. But I don't think I will. I didn't see anything at all."

Cal stood. "Thanks for talking to us."

"Hey, any time. And have you heard anything more about *Dusted*, Quincy? I'd really, really like to be in another one of your movies. I'd love it if they made it a series. Quincy, well, not you, but the character, is so much fun, and you know I love Tiny, both the character and I met the real life one a couple times and liked her, too."

"I haven't heard for sure," I told her. "But as soon as I do, we'll call."

"Thanks, Quincy. And thank for giving me the opportunity. Some people look at me and just see a reality show star. You saw me as so much more."

Now, here's the thing, I did go to bat for Jonas playing Cal, but I didn't know anything about Shia before they said she was up for the role of Tiny. I didn't protest, but I didn't lobby for her. She seemed nice, but we'd never gotten close like I had with Cilla.

"I'm sure we'll be talking to you soon," I said.

We walked down the stairs, then towards the car. When we got inside, Cal said, "Well, she's. ..." and left the sentence hanging, as if he couldn't think of anything that accurately described Shia.

"She's someone who is entirely herself," I filled in. "I think that's why they picked her for the reality show. She young and has a lot of maturing left to do. She has no inner filter. If she thinks it, she says it. But there's not malice in her. I mean, she'll flirt with any male—I'm pretty sure you were in her sites, Detective Hunky."

"Hey, that's not what she called me and I'm an officially engaged man now, so even if she was blatantly flirting, I wouldn't notice because the only woman I have eyes for is you."

I snorted, though it was sweet of him to say. "You're heading to Jonas's now?"

He nodded.

Jonas lived in a condo. It was a three-story building that was all glass and sleek lines. He lived on the top floor. He opened the door wearing nothing but tight biking shorts and sweat.

"Quincy," he said and hugged me to his bare, sweaty, buff chest.

Cal made a choking noise behind me and Jonas released me immediately. "And Quincy's cop," he added, using his nickname for Cal.

Cal shook Jonas's hand, and I figured he made out on the bargain because Jonas had already wiped most of his sweat on me.

"Sorry for hugging Quincy like that in front of you," he said, then quickly added, "not that I'd be hugging her behind your back like that. I just meant... I mean, I didn't like Mellie, I don't think anyone did, but she worked with us. She was one of us. And now she's dead. And I was there at the party. Quincy's party. I'm just so upset."

"It's okay, Jonas," Cal assured him. "I don't get jealous when other guys hug Quincy because I know she's mine. Just like she knows I'm hers."

I flashed Jonas the ring. "It's official."

"So he finally got you to take it off your chain? I hope it was something romantic."

"She asked me to re-ask her at the murder scene."

Jonas looked at me and shook his head. "Oh, hell, Quincy. This is why you write murder mysteries, not freakin' romance. Seriously, I'm not known for romantic roles, but even I know that after making a guy wait forever to make it official, he deserved to be wined and dined a bit. *You* should have gotten on one knee and—"

Cal shot me that sexy look of his, then said to Jonas, "She could have slipped it on her finger at the corner of Hollywood and Vine, and I'd have been fine because she finally said yes."

Jonas laughed. "Yeah, I figure I'd feel the same if I finally caught a woman like Quincy."

I waved my hand in the air. They were sweet, but they were making me uncomfortable. "Standing here feeling very exposed and wondering if we can turn the talk from me and my lack of romantic proposals to—"

"Mellie," Jonas said. "Yeah. Sorry. Come in, make yourselves at home and give me a sec to throw on a shirt."

He disappeared into the hall and Cal and I sat on the couch.

"Nice guy," I said.

"Or he just played one on TV," Cal quipped.

I laughed and hugged him. "He is kinda right. You deserved a better proposal." He'd proposed to me in front of my family at Christmas—a truly romantic proposal. And I'd accepted at a murder scene.

He must have sensed I was worrying because he gently put his hands on my cheeks and looked me right in the eye. "I proposed to you and having you finally say a definitive *yes* was romantic enough for me."

I gave him a hug. Not for the first time, I realized I was a very lucky woman.

"Okay, actor in the room," Jonas called. "If you keep that up I'll be studying it for future movies. Have you heard officially about *Dusted*?"

"Not yet," I told him, "but you know you'll hear as soon as I do."

He sat down across for us.

"So do you have a white-board set up?"

"Yeah. Two actually," I said.

He nodded, then turned to Cal. "And are you threatening to send her to jail for interfering with your investigation?"

"It's not my investigation."

"Yeah, this time it's a different cop. I talked to him," Jonas said. "Detective Randolph."

Cal nodded. "And I'm officially taking some personal time and working with Quincy this time."

Jonas looked from Cal, to me, then said, "Because you know she'd be looking into this with or without your support." His eyes narrowed as he looked at me. "Because they killed Mellie at your old house, at Peri's house, in your son's room. And even without all that, you'd be taking a look because you knew Mellie. She was in your movie and even if you didn't like her, you feel responsible for her. Like Theresa."

"I do like Theresa," I maintained. "She just wasn't cut out for being a maid. She is a very good office manager."

He nodded. "And Cal, you know Quincy'd be investigating one way or another, and since the murderer implicated her by leaving the body on a bed with a a Mortie Award, you're afraid they're going to come after Quincy, since implicating her didn't work. You want to keep her safe. You're a cop and finding the murderer would generally be your primary focus, but in this case, Quincy is. More than that, she's your only focus. I bet you've let her take the lead role and ask her question, right?"

"Jonas," I said.

Jonas chuckled. "Okay. You're right. Let's get down to what I saw, who I saw, and I'll try to be as detailed as possible in case something little is what this case hinges on."

He rattled off his memories of the evening without my prodding.

"What about Shia?" I asked.

"What about her?"

"Are you two. ..."

"Oh, not even close. Listen, she's a nice girl. She's sort of like what Mellie might have been if Mellie'd had a soul to go with those looks. Shia's sweet but ambitious. And she's not above using people to achieve those ambitions. If we hooked up, then she'd stay in the public's eye even if there's not another movie. I'm not interested in that kind of relationship. I made it clear to both Shia and Mellie. I could try to gloss over the fact Mellie hit on me, too, but I trust you to figure out who did it, and since I didn't, I don't mind telling you she hit on me and hit on me hard throughout the movie, and at your party. I turned her down flat each and every time."

"And how did she take that?" Cal asked.

"About as well as you'd think she would. I told both of them no, but I didn't kill Mellie. And I don't think Shia did either."

"Can you tell us where you were when the cops came in?"

"Me, Shia, Cilla, and Dylan were all talking. Shia's dad came in and joined us. He's so proud of her—that much was apparent. He seemed to feel awkward around us, but he had a drink then left. I thought it was nice to see a father that proud of his kid. My dad wanted me to be a doctor, so I wouldn't say pride was ever his primary emotion about my career."

"Is he a doctor?" I asked.

"Yeah, surgeon." Jonas was wearing an expression I'd seen before...in the mirror.

"God save us from surgeons," I muttered.

Jonas laughed. "Yeah, I will confess, I played Cal in the movie, but I felt a certain sense or camaraderie with you. I get that entire parental expectation thing that you or your character—whichever—experienced. I understood it. I relate."

"Hey, at least you've built a great career."

"I've made my career playing a villain, at least until *Steamed*. That you could see me as something more than a blow-'em-up, shoot-'em-up kind of actor...Well, it meant more to me than you'll ever know."

Cal cleared his throat.

Jonas laughed at Cal's annoyed expression and said, "Dude, you should probably know that if you ever screw up there are lot of men in the wings who would snap her up."

"Again, I'm here and feeling uncomfortable," I said.

It was one thing to flirt with Big G, who I knew was only flirting to annoy Cal. It was entirely another thing to have Jonas flirt with me. I wasn't quite sure what to do about it. Part of me was flattered, but the main part of me wasn't interested and didn't enjoy the banter.

"I'll stop. But if he ever hurts you, you know my number." Jonas shot me a killer smile which made Cal annoyed. He didn't have to say anything for me to realize that.

Getting back to business, I asked, "Okay, so can you think of anything else from that night? Anything that sticks out, even if it seems insignificant?"

"I know that Cilla and Dylan had a fight, but not in an I'll-go-kill-Mellie-now sort of way. It was just a couple sort of disagreement. I don't know what about. And I mention it in case someone else did and you're looking at them. It wasn't them."

"I don't think so either."

"And... well, anything I say will stay between us, right?"

"I told Detective Randolph I'd share anything that was relevant to the case, but if it's not, sure, we'll keep it between us."

"Mellie hit on me again, big time. Blatantly at your party. She '*accidentally*,'" he air-quoted the word, "let the strap fall and let the bodice of that tart-fest dress she was wearing slip in order to expose herself. Then laughed, pulled up the strap and whispered that the dress obviously wanted the same thing she wanted."

He shook his head in disgust. "I explained that both her and the dress were out of luck."

"That sounds like Mellie," I said.

I didn't like her before, but my dislike had grown as I talked to people. I felt bad about that. I didn't like not liking a dead woman.

"I didn't kill her because she hit on me," Jonas said. "I mean, I've been hit on a few times in the past and the women I turned down are all still alive.

"Thanks, Jonas."

"You'll keep me posted?" he asked.

I wasn't sure if he wanted me to keep him posted on the investigation or on whether or not *Dusted* was going to be produced, but it didn't matter. I nodded.

"We'll talk to you soon," Cal said and stood.

I followed suit.

"Are you going to the memorial service?"

I felt horrible. I hadn't thought about Mellie's service. I didn't like her, but there was no way I could not go.

"Yes, I'm sure I'll have to go." It sounded less than enthused even to my own ears. "Sorry. But yes, I'll be there."

"Me, too. I think maybe that's the saddest part of this whole thing. I mean, everyone dies, but it would be nice to think when it's your time to go, people will mourn you. But I guess, you reap what you sow." He paused. "And yes, I know how that sounded. *Reap What You Sow*. Now there's a title in that."

He saw us to the door. "Speaking of titles," he said before we walked out. If you write a screenplay based on this, you should call it *Swept Up*. Like swept up in all the Hollywood glitz and glamour, or even swept up in your engagement to Cal. But if you want an actor's perspective before you write it, make your proposal to Cal more romantic in the screenplay, and make the *Mellie character* more likeable. Even if no one's going to really mourn her at her memorial, your audience will mourn her character on the screen."

He hugged me again. "That was just to watch the big guy get all snarly. I wanted to be sure I had the expression down for the next movie." And he did do a masterful impression of Cal's growl. I know, because I'd been on that receiving end of it more than once.

"Talk to you soon," he said and shut the door as we walked down the hall to the elevator.

"So did you get all worried when the big, hunky, sweaty, buff man hugged me?"

"I trust you," he said, which really didn't answer my question. "Of course, I don't trust him at all."

I laughed and took his hand.

CHAPTER SEVEN

DETECTIVE CHARLIE CALLED first thing on Thursday. I suggested we meet at Pattycake's, the local pancake house, but he asked if we could meet at my place. He wanted to take a look at my white-board and see what I had.

I reluctantly said yes.

I hung up the phone and scurried around the house trying to clean up before he arrived. It was one of the few times since moving to LA that I was happy about the traffic situation. I hoped it was horrible today and slowed him up.

"Cal, seriously, you're worse than the boys," I called as I picked up a pair of his socks from under the couch.

First off, that was a lie. My boys were much, much worse than Cal. When I move them into their dorm rooms I went up and helped them settle. Then I never went back until it was time to move them out—at least not after I went up to Hunter's room once. I never repeated that mistake with him or his younger brothers. They were that bad.

I didn't feel guilty about lying to Cal though, because secondly, who takes off their socks on the couch? I take mine off in a bedroom or the bathroom when I change clothes, but seriously, I don't believe I've ever left a pair of socks languishing under my couch.

"Quincy, calm down," Cal said from the hall. I'd asked him to clean the bathroom.

"Calm down? I invited your cop buddy to Pattycake's, but he wanted to come here."

"You could have said no," Cal said, oh so reasonably. "After all, you said no to me that first time."

"Yeah, but I promised Charlie I'd cooperate with him…I didn't promise you that."

Still trying to be the soul of reasonableness, Cal tried, "I don't think he's going to check under the couch."

Cal might be wonderful, he might be smart and have great intuition, but seriously he still hadn't figured out not to mess with a woman in the midst of a cleaning frenzy?

"But what if he did check under the couch?" I asked. "I'm a maid, and I have a reputation. I have professional pride. Between the Mortie Awards and then the investigation, the house is looking a bit rough."

"You're nuts. You know that, right?"

I hurried down the hall and kissed him. "That's what you love about me."

He snorted, then kissed me back.

That kiss could easily have become something more if I didn't have Detective Charlie on his way over.

"Later," I whispered and pulled away. "Back to cleaning."

Cal sighed.

After he finished, I took pity on him and asked him to make a donut run.

"Just because he's a cop doesn't mean he likes donuts," he pointed out.

"You're right, but it doesn't mean he doesn't. You're a cop and you like donuts."

"Not because I'm a cop," he maintained stubbornly.

"No, because you're human. I mean, who doesn't like donuts?"

He left without another word.

Ten minutes later, Detective Charlie arrived ... early.

"You're early," I said by way of a greeting.

"I'm normally early. I'm never late." He waited half a beat, then asked, "Can I come in?"

I opened the door and let him in. I couldn't help but remember the first time Cal had tried to come in my house to ask my about Mr. Banning's murder scene. I smiled.

Charlie noticed. "What?"

"I was just remembering the first time Cal came over."

"You slammed the door in his face and wouldn't let him in." I must have looked surprised, because he added by way of an explanation. "The movie."

I shut the door and beckoned him. I led him into the now straightened up living room with the two big whiteboards in it.

"Wow, you've been busy," he said.

"Want some coffee? Cal will be back home any minute with donuts."

"I don't like donuts because I'm a cop," he groused, echoing Cal's words.

"No, but you do because you're human. What's not to love? We have a donut shop in Erie, *Mighty Fine*, that makes the best donuts ever. But *Danny's Donuts* here in LA is a close second."

"Believe it or not, your mom mentioned *Mighty Fine* when I called her. She'd stopped to buy them for her office. She said the same thing."

"A corroborating witness," I teased.

I thought he had a hint of a smile as he answered, "I take my coffee black."

"Of course you do," I said and turned to get it, but the doorbell stopped me in my tracks. "I'll be right back."

I opened the door, doubly thankful I'd cleaned, and found Tiny and Sal. "Hey, what's up?" I opened the door and let them in only to be scooped into Tiny's arms.

I'd had an inordinate amount of hugs lately.

"I'm pregnant,' she said, loudly, in my ear. "Knocked up. With child. Expecting." She squeezed me tightly. "There's so much to do and only six months left to do it. I don't think pregnancy lasts long enough. Why, I have to decorate the nursery and shop. Not just for clothes, but for a baptism gown and—"

"Breathe," Sal said.

Tiny released me and I turned to hug Sal. Then looked at them both. "Congratulations."

I might not be a hugger by nature, but the hug I gave her was totally necessary.

"And of course you'll be the baby's godmother," she said. "So you'll have to get a dress for the baptism, too. We've got so much to do. ..."

And she launched into the list that was evolving and expanding as she went.

I wanted to ask them to come in.

Offer them something to drink.

To be honest, I wanted to distract Tiny from her baby-planning. I'd been down this road when she'd been planning her wedding to Sal. Months of walking into her office to find myself in a sea of pastel taffeta.

"Tiny," Sal finally said firmly.

"Okay, okay, I know. I'll stop."

"Detective Charlie's here. I was just getting him coffee. Cal will be back any minute with donuts."

"I can't have coffee—"

"I'll bring you milk." I looked at Sal. "You?"

"Coffee. And there's a tip in it if you make it an Irish coffee."

I laughed, because I knew he wasn't serious. Then Tiny rushed in and told Detective Charlie she was pregnant and started on her to-do list again, and Sal shot me a look that said he might be serious about the alcohol in his coffee after all.

I smiled. "The beautiful thing about your wife is she never does anything by halves. It's why we have a successful business. And it's why you have her. She got you in her sites and you didn't stand a chance."

He laughed. "You're right."

I brought out everyone's drinks, Cal arrived with donuts and after Tiny told him about the baby and wound down, he stood next to Charlie, pointing out things on the board. I felt torn between Tiny and Sal, and Charlie and Cal.

"We should probably let the three of you get down to all your murder talk," Tiny said.

"Unless you need legal representation," Sal teased me.

"I don't, but you two don't have to leave. I haven't found anything. No, conflicting statements. No clues. Nothing. I really think those first two times were flukes."

Before Tiny could jump in and say something to comfort me, Detective Charlie said, "You've made progress. Your boards show well thought out, well-documented timelines, and suspect assessments."

"I'm biased," I admitted. "I mean, I never even entertained the thoughts of Tiny or Sal here having done it so I took them right off the suspect list."

Tiny piped up, "That other woman, Shia, she hit on Sal. But I didn't kill her, so I can't imagine I'd have a motive to kill Mellie. Although, to be fair, detective, I didn't like her either. Not that I knew her well, but what I did know, I didn't like. Mac'Cleaner's does a lot of work for Hollywood types. Most of our clients are decent people. But I've noticed the actors on the lower end of the food chain are the biggest pitas."

"Pitas?" he asked.

"Pains-in-the … uh, butts," I answered.

"Yeah, I've met my share of those," Charlie admitted, "and I'm sure Cal has, too. From what I've learned about Mellie, I wouldn't have liked her either. But not liking someone has never been a very good motive for murder, in my experience."

"Mine either," Cal said. "Though, hating someone is more of one. And loving them. People with strong emotions on either end of the scale are more prone to killing."

"My only experience was Mr. Banning," I said, "and that strong love/hate thing certainly applied."

"Then I'm out," Tiny said. "I didn't like her, but I didn't know her well enough to feel more than mild annoyance."

"We're not really any closer to an answer," I said with a sigh.

"We could be, we just don't know it yet. We need that one crucial piece of the puzzle, then everything else we've gathered will fall in to place," Charlie said. "Do you have anything else you want to share with me?"

"You heard about the memorial service on Saturday?"

"I did. I'll be there."

"Us, too," I said indicating Cal.

"Not us," Sal said. "Unless you need us."

"I think we're good. I just want to solve this and get back to my normal life."

"Oh, Quincy, there won't be any normal for a while," Tiny gushed. "We have your wedding and the baby to plan for."

Oh, no. I thought the baby might have pushed thoughts of my wedding from her head.

"Your mom's coming in town in two weeks so the three of us can get to work," she continued. "There's so much to do. Finding a venue and cake, and let's not even talk about your wedding dress. And. ..."

I groaned.

"But the baby," I tried. "You have to plan for the baby."

"Quincy, I can do both," she assured me.

I wasn't sure I could.

Later that day, Cal and I were still making calls when my phone rang. I dropped my pen on my notepad—my overflowing with notes and recordings—when I saw it was Detective Charlie. He called to tell me that the coroner had ruled on Mellie's cause of death. I waited for the words, *blunt force trauma*, but instead he said, "Strangulation."

"Strangulation?" I asked. There had been no blood at this crime, but I hadn't felt that ruled out her getting whacked with the Mortie. It only meant that the wound hadn't bled.

"How hard would it be for a woman to strangle someone?" I asked.

Cal was on the phone with someone, but was obviously listening well enough that he shot me a look. I defended the question. "I don't think I'm being gender biased when I say that women don't have the upper body strength that men do. I don't know how hard it is to strangle someone with a...what did they use?"

"Bare hands," Charlie said. "They shattered Mellie's trachea."

I was pretty sure that ruled out most, if not all the females on my list.

Charlie agreed.

"Well, thank you for letting me know. And the Mortie?"

"As far as we can tell, it was placed in her hands after the fact."

"So we were right, they were trying to make us take a look at either me, or the movie."

"I think so," he agreed.

Not a woman. Someone who wanted the cops looking at me, or the movie. "Okay," I said and hung up.

So, why would someone want the cops looking at me, or the movie? Maybe because whoever killed Mellie didn't have anything to do with the movie and wanted to point the cops in that way because it was the wrong direction?

Cal was just finishing up his call when I hung up. I filled him in.

Cal listened and got very serious. "Quincy, I know that we tend to spend some time at our own places and not sleep over—I hate saying that I sound like I'm a ten-year-old girl planning a slumber party. Anyway, I know that I should probably make some move to go home tonight, but I don't want to leave you until we find out who killed Mellie and they're in custody."

"I've been thinking about that. ..." I said.

"And?"

"When you asked me to marry you, I asked for time. Time on my own to get to know myself. Well, I've had my time. And I know I'm better when you're with me. So it's stupid for you to go home every night or two. The truth is, I don't find any great insights into myself when you're gone ... I just miss you."

"What are you saying?" he asked cautiously.

"Why don't you move in with me? I mean, we haven't talked about where we'll live after we're married, and if you'd rather we can look for some place totally new for both of us, but for now, my place is bigger than yours, so we could live here."

"If you want a new place, we can look, but I'm fine with here. Quincy, I'm fine living pretty much anywhere, as long as you're there."

I know it wasn't champagne and caviar. And my proposal wasn't that either. But for me, his last sentence was one of the most romantic things anyone had ever said to me.

Wow. The last week had brought about a lot of changes in my life. I was officially engaged. I'd won a Mortie for my screenplay. I'd found another dead body. My best friend was having a baby, and I was going to be a godmother. And now I was living with someone ... officially.

Now, if we could just find the murderer, it would be a very good week indeed.

The next day, Cal had to go to a hearing for a guy he'd busted a while back. He could have said he was taking personal time and got the court date pushed back, but he didn't want to.

I knew his hesitancy to go wasn't that he was worried about me working on the investigation and not filling him in—it was that he was worried about me.

"Go," I told him. "My only plans for the day are to reread everything we've gathered and maybe got to *Psst* for lunch."

"Nowhere else?" he asked.

"Honey made a new dish and invited Peri and me to try it."

"You'll be with Peri?" he asked.

I nodded. "I will." I wasn't sure what he thought Peri would do if some big, bad murderer came after me. I wasn't sure what he thought she'd do if a mouse came after me. Or a bug. Peri didn't have any killer instincts.

Peri and Jerome still hadn't been allowed to move back into their home. They were staying at Le Celebre Hotel—which was home to Honey's restaurant, Psst—so it was very convenient.

"Don't forget, we're partners in this," he reminded me, as if I needed reminding. "Talk to Honey, and to any of her staff that are there, but nowhere else, no one else without me."

I knew what he was really saying was, *I'm afraid for you. I love you. Don't get yourself killed.*

I mock-spit in my hand and crossed my heart. The boys used to do that all the time when they were younger.

Only they didn't mock spit.

Reluctantly, Cal left.

I did some laundry and reread all my notes. I'd become a copious note-taker. When Mr. Banning died, everything seemed so vivid—so much bolder than real life. I figured there was no way I'd forget a single second of it.

Then I started writing the screenplay and realized how much of the detail was hazy.

Determined to have a complete record of Mellie's murder I'd been diligent this time. My notepad was full, and I'd taped a number of conversations.

Somewhere in all those notes, there had to be something I'd missed.

But I couldn't find it.

At noon, with details swimming through my head like some macabre film, I put the files away and headed over to Le Celebre Hotel. I went up to the Presidential Suite.

Peri opened the door.

"Don't say a word about this. ..." She waved her hand at the stately, opulent room. "I told Jerome we should just stay with you, he said it was weird rooming with an ex-wife. I pointed out you were more than that, you were the mother of his children and my friend. He wouldn't listen. So, I agreed when he wanted to move out. I thought we'd be in a normal hotel room, but Quincy, this is ten times bigger than my first apartment. Not to name drop or anything, but George—"

"George?" I asked.

"Gorgeous George. Come on, Quincy, he played a doctor on television and his his aunt was a famous singer. Hollywood's Gorgeous George."

"Oh." I didn't want to point out there were other George's in Hollywood, because I'd have to admit none were quite as gorgeous as he is.

"Yeah ... oh," Peri said. "He has stayed here. I don't have a lot of Hollywood crushes, but him I might crush on a bit. Do you think that he might play Julian in *Dusted*? Oh, he'd make a perfect Julian. And of course, you'd get to know him and could introduce me."

"Peri, I don't know for sure *Dusted* is going to sell, and I think your George might make more than a movie airing on the HeartMark Channel can afford."

She sighed. "Well, a girl can dream."

"How about dreaming on your way down to the restaurant?" I teased. "If we're late, Honey will be annoyed. She's preparing this just for us."

"Let's go."

Honey Martin was a good friend. Her daughter, Beatrix, aka Trixie—for all you Trixie Belden fans, their names make me smile, too—was Mile's age. We'd commiserated a lot about being the mothers of college-age children.

We walked down to the lobby level and into *Psst.*

"Well, if it isn't our own Quincy Mac, award winning screenwriter and super-sleuth extraordinaire," Honey shouted when she spotted us.

"I wish I was doing more screenwriting and less sleuthing this week," I muttered. Peri must have heard me because she wrapped her arm around mine and led me into Honey's kitchen. Everything was white and stainless steel. It was as bright and shiny as Honey.

"I set a table for you back here, so that I could sit with you."

Honey's an artist. I'm never exactly sure what she's serving me, but it's always beautifully presented and it's always amazing to eat.

Today's dish, according to Honey, was a sandwich.

I looked at the plate she set in front of me and said, "I'm the mother of three boys, and I've made thousands of sandwiches, and this is to those what a hamburger is to filet mignon."

The sandwich was pretty. Paper-thin bread stuffed with some sort of salady thing sitting on a bed of some kind of coleslaw thing. A red sauce was drizzled all over the place, and a small fruit salad ringed the entire presentation.

"I wanted something that was gluten free as well as vegan. Something that would. ..."

Peri had already popped her first bite in her mouth and said, "Wow."

Honey clapped her hand. "That was exactly the reaction that I wanted."

We ate and I asked Honey to run through her recollections of the party. She had a unique perspective. She was there as a guest, but I'd already heard that she'd pitched in and overseen the bar and food. I learned while investigating Mr. Banning's murder that service people are invisible—well, I didn't actually learn it then. As someone who'd built her career in the service industry, I knew it from personal experience well before Mr. Banning.

And even though Honey had been a guest, I thought there was a good chance she wasn't noticed when she was behind the bar.

"I knew a lot of the people, but not all. No one did anything that really stood out. The girl who played you and her husband had a fight. They were giving each other the cold shoulder for a while."

"Did you see Mellie at all?" I asked as I took another bite.

"A couple times. I saw when she came into the party. No one seemed happy to see her. I saw her drape herself over almost every available man at the party, but none of them seemed overly inclined to take her blatant offers. And I already told Detective Randolph that I saw her talking to one guy I didn't know. They were on the other side of the room, so I didn't get a good look at him, but it was close enough that I'd have recognized him if I knew him. I could tell Mellie had a cat-who-ate-the-canary sort of look, but he wasn't happy at all. Detective Randolph said he's bringing over pictures of everyone on the guest list later. I know it wasn't anyone on the catering staff."

I pulled out my cellphone and opened the file where I'd stashed all the guests' pictures.

She thumbed through the photos as I finished the meal and said, "If I could live in a world where you or Big G cooked for me every night, life would be perfect."

She stopped thumbing through the pictures and looked up at me. "I'm going out with him. I hope you don't mind."

I glanced at the picture on my phone. "Jonas?"

She shook her head. "No Big G."

"Why would I mind? That's delightful news." To be honest, they were perfect for each other.

Peri put down her fork and clapped her hands. "Oh, that's wonderful. Quincy and I decided a while back the two of you were perfect for each other. You both like food. You're both nice. And—"

Honey held up her hand. "He is nice. And do you know, he's read all the Trixie Belden books."

Now, Big G was many things, but I'd never imagined that he was a fan of teen girl mysteries.

"Your expression is priceless," Honey said, laughing. "He read them when he was a kid and was laid up with a broken leg one summer. His sister had the collection. He was so cute when he told me he never felt emasculated by how much he liked them. He claims they were manly in their own way, that there were enough major male characters that he felt they could be guy-reads."

"So he enjoyed the fact that Beatrix is called Trixie?"

She nodded. "That's how the conversation started. He realized the connection in our names."

She started scanning through the pictures again. "I don't see him."

"I haven't got everyone's picture yet. Let me check out NetMovieDatabase and Facebook to see if I can find pictures of the dozen or so people I don't have yet. Can I text them to you?"

"Sure."

Peri grinned as we left *Psst*. "Honey saw a strange man talking to Mellie. That has to be him. I just knew it wasn't someone we knew and liked."

"That would be too simple. A strange man sneaks into your house and murders a woman who no one liked, then snuck out again without anyone being the wiser?" It was the perfect scenario, but I didn't think someone with no connection to us killed Mellie. It would make things simpler though.

And sometimes the simplest answer was the best one. *Occam's Razor.* Hey, I don't just watch detective shows, I watch *Big Bang*, too. And we all felt that the Mortie in Mellie's hand was a distraction. It made sense that someone who wasn't connected to the movie wanted us to look at the movie.

"Yes. A stranger. Quincy, your friends are my friends, and I worked with the cast and crew. The only person at the party who I think might be capable of murder was Mellie."

I had to agree.

"Do you have any more investigating to do today?" Peri asked.

"No. I promised Cal. You, then lunch with Honey, then home. He's trying to pretend that he's my trusty sidekick in this investigation, but he really sees himself as my bodyguard. He's convinced that whoever killed Mellie might come after me."

"Why?" she asked.

"The Mortie. It was too much like Mr. Banning's murder. We think it's a distraction. Someone put it there to have the cops concentrating on me and the movie."

"Maybe you have a deranged fan. Jerome made that movie last year about the actress with the deranged fan. And there's that Kathy Bates movie. I love Kathy Bates. She's one of my favorite actors."

"I like her, too, but frankly, I wouldn't want her or anyone else to be my deranged fan."

"But think of the screenplay you'd get out of that? Dick would be thrilled."

I laughed. "He would."

"So, listen, since you're not allowed to investigate, I have an idea…"

"…and I will never listen to another one of Peri's ideas again," I told Cal that night. "But before I knew it, she'd called Tiny and they dragged me to the bridal shop."

"Oh, the horrors," Cal exclaimed in a mocking sort of way.

"It was. They called Mom and then texted her pictures as I tried on dresses. They've all agreed that a traditional white Cinderella gown won't do. But none of them could agree on what they think I should wear."

"What do you think you should wear?" he asked in a much more supportive way.

"Jeans and a Mac'Cleaner's sweatshirt?" I asked.

He laughed, as if he thought I was joking. "You'll survive."

"You think?"

"Quincy, clothes are clothes. Whether you're wearing a gown or jeans, you're still the most beautiful woman I've ever seen."

Now, this was sweet. You'd think that I'd be all swoony and melty. And I was a bit, but Cal's cavalier *clothes-are-clothes* attitude nettled a bit, so I shared my mother's offer with relish.

"I'm so glad you feel that way, *darling*." Now we rarely use terms of endearments. He's Cal. Occasionally Caleb. I'm Quincy. Occasionally Quince. So that *darling* caught his attention.

"Mom decided that I need something unique," I said with relish. "And given that I'd named Mac'Cleaners after our actual family name, she had a brilliant idea. All the Mac men would wear kilts. They all have them. She was ordering a Mclean kilt for you before I even got home."

His clothes-are-just-clothes expression disappeared and was replaced with horror. "Wait, what?"

"Yes. She wanted you and all the Mac men to wear kilts to our wedding. Sporrans even."

"What's a sporran?" he asked.

I could hear the trepidation in his voice. And while I loved the man like crazy, I will confess, I did sort of enjoy picking on him more than might be considered seemly.

"That little purse guys wear over their," I gestured at the bodily region the sporran covered.

"A man purse?"

"A man purse that tends to sit right...." I graphically pointed this time.

"I take back what I said. Clothes do matter. Let's just elope. You can wear jeans and your Mac'Cleaner's sweatshirt. I'll wear the same, too for that matter."

"It's too late, buddy. Mom, Tiny, and Peri have their little fingers in this particular wedding cake. There's nothing we can do. Honey's already planning our menu."

"I think I'm going to have to wear my family's traditional wedding garb," he said.

"Parker is English. Your mom was a Baeur. You want to wear lederhosen?"

He sighed. "No."

"Mom will be thrilled you decided to embrace our family tradition."

"You're enjoying this," he accused.

"No. But hey, if I have to suffer, I think you should, too."

"I think we're going to have to have a serious talk about what kind of wedding we want."

I hugged him. "Don't tell my mom, Tiny, or Peri, but the only thing that really matters to me is that you're there."

"Me, too," he said sweetly. But I couldn't miss the fact that he mumbled, "But it would be nice if I didn't have to wear a kilt.

CHAPTER EIGHT

O N SATURDAY, I decided to wear black to Mellie's memorial service. I sucked in my stomach as I looked at myself in the mirror and immediately felt vain that something like my baby pooch should bother me when I was on the way to a funeral.

Then I felt worse because I was wearing black to Mellie's funeral.

I didn't know her well, and what I did know I didn't like. So looking like I was in mourning made me feel disingenuous.

But I decided to keep the black dress on. I might not have liked Mellie, but I didn't wish her dead, so I could mourn the fact that someone lost their life too soon. I guess I was mourning the fact that she'd never have a chance to be the person she could have been.

I was mourning the loss of her potential.

I felt a bit less fake as I walked out into the living room and found Cal in a dark, navy suit.

"You look nice," I told him.

"So do you," he said.

Now most of the time if either of us said something like that, we'd have done that particular little eyebrow wiggle that indicated how we'd like to celebrate our looking-niceness. But we were both somber because it was a funeral.

There was no eyebrow wiggling. No suggestive looks or comments.

We were a somber duo as we headed out to the memorial.

"Charlie called and interviewed all three boys. They didn't have anything to share with him. Neither did my family or Lottie." I voiced my inner fear. "We're not getting anywhere, Cal."

"We'll figure it out, Quincy. It hasn't even been a week."

"Almost. Last week at this time we were getting ready for the Morties. I was so excited. I know they always say it's an honor to simply be nominated, and it's so true…it was. I kept wanting to pinch myself."

"I know."

I was quiet, mulling and then said, "Peri said they released the crime scene. She and Jerome are moving back into the house today."

"That's good."

"Cal, Peri said my Mortie will be there. I'm not sure what I'm going to do with it, even if it wasn't mine, but rather Sean's Mortie they found with Mellie."

"Quincy," Cal said. Just my name. But I could hear his love and support in it.

"It doesn't seem right to put it on the shelf."

"You might not want to display it right away, but you will."

I didn't know about that.

The church was a sea of blacks, grays, and dark blue, but I didn't see anyone crying.

That was a sad legacy. When I died, I'd like people to say I'd had a good life, but I wouldn't mind a tear or two.

As the minister gave his eulogy, I looked through the audience. People from *Steamed*, as well as other industry people, filled the seats.

Cilla and Dylan sat a few rows away from us. She leaned into him. I took it as a sign that all was well between them.

Shia sat with her father. He had his arm draped over her shoulder.

I noticed that Jonas wasn't sitting anywhere near her. He was on the other side of the church, sitting with Vinny Weindorf, who'd played Sal. I hadn't talked to Vinny. He hadn't been at the party, so I was sure he hadn't seen anything that night, but he'd been on set with her. He might have seen something there.

I'd track him down at the wake.

My agent, Deanne, was there. I wondered how she knew Mellie. Of course, she'd been in the industry for years. She knew most everyone, and those she didn't know personally she knew of.

No one other than the minister said any words.

I felt bad about that, too.

When the minister finished, everyone left quietly, orderly, and quickly. There was no lingering, no hugs of comfort.

The wake was at Le Celebre Hotel...in the small ballroom. Honey's *Psst* was catering. She pulled me aside as we entered. "Quincy, I heard a bit of gossip. Normally, I wouldn't pass it on, but given that Mellie is dead, and knowing you won't say anything to anyone else...."

She left the sentence hanging, as if waiting for me to confirm that I wouldn't, so I nodded.

"Mellie had just broken up with someone and broken up meanly. Rumor has it that she had thought he'd cast her in his next show, and what he did was cast her aside."

"Then he broke up with her?" I asked.

"Well, first, but she broke up second in a very public venue," Honey said.

"Where?"

"Here, at the hotel. He was meeting with someone and she walked up to the table, dumped a glass of red wine on him, then said some horrible, emasculating things, and told him they were over. He tried to protest that he'd already said as much. And...."

"And?" I prompted.

"And the rumor said that her parting words were, '*The only way anyone will ever break up with me is over my dead body.*'"

"Oh," I said. I know, it wasn't a very detectivey sounding response, but I'm not a detective. I don't even play one on TV.

"You didn't say who the red-wine-wearing person was." I realized that this wasn't a good sign. There was a very good chance that whoever she said was going to be someone that I knew. And I had a sinking feeling that the fact she hadn't said meant I wasn't going to be happy about it.

"Dick."

"Pardon?" She couldn't mean who I thought she meant.

"Dick Macy. Your friend. Your mentor."

"Dick and Mellie?" I didn't see it. I couldn't see it. Dick had dated a few women since we'd met. Nice women. Normal women. Mellie was neither.

"Quincy, I didn't see any of this for myself. It was a few weeks back and one of my staff mentioned it because she knows we're friends and she's a fan. She recognized Mellie, but she didn't know the man's name. After she heard the news reports, she looked up the receipt and it the meal was charged to Richard Macy's card."

Dick had come over. We'd talked. He'd asked about the investigation, but he'd never said a word about this.

"Quincy, I'm sorry, but I thought you should know."

"You were right to tell me, Honey."

"I don't think it means anything," she said. "I've met Dick. He's a nice guy. He's started coming here on occasion. He always compliments the chef."

"He is a nice guy." But I'd learned from a lot from my television series addiction.

Sometimes nice guys did it.

I felt horrible. Guilty before the fact, because I knew immediately that I wasn't gong to say anything about Honey's rumor to Cal. It was just a rumor. I'd ask Dick about it and he'd laugh it off. He'd have some logical explanation, I was sure.

"You okay?" Cal asked when I rejoined him.

I nodded, but the fact I'd decided not to tell him about Dick weighed on me. I felt sick with the silence.

"Let's make the rounds and see if anyone has remembered anything, or inadvertently says something."

And we did. We circled around the room.

No one said anything incriminating. The thing that stood out for me the most was how no one said much about Mellie period.

Most wakes I'd gone to, people shared memories and stories of the deceased. This time they spoke about anything but.

I bumped into Sean, whose Mortie for best director of a made-for-television movie had been clutched by Mellie's dead hands. I'd called him twice, hoping to talk to him, but he hadn't returned my calls. I spotted him in the corner and glanced at Cal, who saw him, too. We both meandered in his direction.

"Hi, Sean. You remember my fiancé, Cal, right?"

He thrust out his hand and the men shook.

"You okay?" I asked.

"I know you called me to ask me about Mellie. The cops have been all over me, too. I'll tell you what I told them. I didn't have an affair with her. I'd left the Mortie up in the room when I'd changed out of my tux and into jeans. I didn't do it, I don't know who did do it. Sure, she was a pain in the *butt.*" He didn't say butt, but I'd made a practice of editing swearwords from my head and my mouth for years. I substituted without thinking.

"But Quincy, I've worked with bigger pains over the years. She never hit on me, and I can assure you that I'd never hit on her. She was decidedly not my type."

I'd met Sean's wife. She was a small bundle of energy with a huge smile. I'd liked her instantly, so I had to agree, Mellie wouldn't have been his type.

"Why didn't you return my calls?" I asked.

"Honestly?"

Cal gave him a cop look. "Honestly."

"I loved *Steamed*, and I'm hoping to work on *Dusted*. But you're not a cop. I'd rather leave the investigation up to the actual police."

He shot Cal a nervous look. "I know you're a cop, but the other Detective said you're taking personal time to keep an eye on Quincy."

"Hey, Cal took time off to work with me," I said, though I knew Sean was right…he was watching out for me more than detecting.

The men gave each other a look, but didn't include me in it. "I don't need looking after, I just needed you to call me back," I insisted.

"There's one more reason I didn't call you back," Sean said. "I seriously don't want to end up in your next script. I'm a behind the camera guy, not a character."

I couldn't help it, I laughed. "Yeah, I get that."

"So, you're not going to demand I don't direct *Dusted*?" he asked.

"No, if everything works out, I'd ask for you to direct again, not that what I say goes."

I could see him visibly relax. "Thanks. I told that Detective Randolph I'd left my Mortie in my bag upstairs. I didn't like Mellie—no one did—and I was thankful her character wouldn't be in *Dusted*. Like I said, she hadn't hit on me, and I certainly didn't hit on her. I think my Mortie being there was just lucky happenstance for the murderer. It's not like everyone and their brother doesn't know that there was a Mortie involved with *Steamed*."

I nodded. "Okay."

Sean looked at Cal, who nodded as well.

"It was my first Mortie," Sean said. "I'm not sure what to do with it, and I feel awful for feeling awful it was involved."

"Don't feel bad. I asked if it was mine." That wasn't my proudest moment.

"You did?" he asked.

I nodded. "I did. And even though it wasn't, mine feels... tainted."

"That makes me feel better," Sean said. He beat a hasty retreat. I think he was still nervous about annoying me.

Cal and I continued through the room. No one said anything else of interest. A few people got a bit tipsy. A few more got more than just a bit. The *few-more* included some guy I'd never met and Shia, who was happily sitting on his lap... when she wasn't practically sliding off it.

Dylan wobbled as he came over with Cilla.

They both had happy drunk expressions on their faces.

"Do I need to take your keys?" I teased.

"Maybe his but not mine," Cilla assured me and they both laughed.

It took a moment for me to realize what she was saying. Cal, ever the detective, got there sooner. "So the argument was a moot point."

"The mootest. And she's the cutest," Dylan quipped.

"Nothing's certain. I peed on one of those early response tests. There's a lot that could go wrong and. ..." Cilla started.

Dylan wrapped her in his arms. "Nothing's going wrong, babe. It's all smooth sailing for us."

She rolled her eyes in his direction, though she was still grinning. "Dylan is obviously planning to take advantage of having a designated driver for a few months."

"Just tonight," he said.

"It makes me sad in a way." Cilla sighed.

"Why?" I asked.

"Sitting at the funeral I couldn't help but feel sad. I mean, I didn't like Mellie, but her death was a waste. Maybe if she'd met the right man, she'd have become a better person. She'll never have that chance now. She'll never have the chance to find someone who would mourn her. Did you notice there was no family here? That's sad."

"She didn't have anyone," I said. It was one of the facts I'd gleaned from NMD and other media sites. "It was just her and her mom, and her mom's dead."

"That's even sadder," Cilla said.

Cilla and Dylan swore us to secrecy, and I told her to call if she had questions. I didn't mention it, but if *Dusted* sold and she was back as Quincy, having had a baby would lend a bit of authenticity to the role.

I thought about checking on Shia, since she was obviously so drunk, but I saw her father leading her out of the ballroom and knew she had a way home.

Cal saw them, too. "I was going to go check on her," he said.

I took his hand and squeezed it.

"What was that for?" he asked.

"You really are a hero. A genuinely nice, caring guy."

"Well, at least I've got that going for me, because I'm not feeling like much of a detective. There were no leads here," Cal said.

I thought about what Honey said and almost told him. Almost.

I promised myself I'd tell him … after I talked to Dick.

But as I drove home with my fiancé, I felt guilty.

And despite that, I still didn't say a word.

It made me wonder just what kind of person Cal was engaged to.

CHAPTER NINE

I CALLED DICK FROM home that night and made arrangements to meet him the next morning for coffee in order to discuss a character issue—I didn't mention the character I wanted to discuss was him.

I called in front of Cal, which meant when I left Sunday morning for Pattycake's, he didn't even question me—so it wasn't a lie.

I was skirting the truth maybe but not lying.

So why did I feel so guilty?

I was sitting at a corner booth towards the back when Dick came in and waved at me.

I'd brought my laptop to add an air of legitimacy to the meeting.

As soon as Dick had his coffee, he said, "So which character is giving you problems?"

I looked at him.

My mentor.

My friend.

Even my partner when I investigated the stolen paintings.

I said, "I have a character who the heroine adores."

I forced myself to continue. "They're very good friends and she'd trust him with her life. The problem is, it's a one-sided friendship. He's at a murder scene in this story and when she asks him about it, he either lies outright or omits some very important information. Either way, it's hard for her to have the whole picture. Why would he do that? I think I'm pretty good at getting into my characters' heads, but I just can't manage it with him. I can't figured out why he'd lie to me … her."

Dick sighed. "I figured you'd find out. I planned to tell you, but just you. I didn't want to tell Cal."

I didn't expect that. "I thought you and Cal were friends, too."

"We are. But. …" He took a long sip of coffee. It had to have burned, but he didn't even wince. He set it back down on table with an audible thud. "Quincy, you and I both know, I'm not the most handsome of men."

"Dick, you're—"

"Don't," he said sharply. "Don't talk about my good personality or other charms. For the most part, I'm happy with who I am. I have a job I love, I have good friends, and I really enjoy running workshops for new writers. I know, some people hate that kind of thing, but I like teaching and fostering young talent. But I am not a handsome man. Women don't swoon when I walk in a room. And Cal … We are friends, but Quincy, not only is he a good looking man—and I mean that in a totally heterosexual way. But he's also a cop. He's accustomed to women swooning. So talking about this in front of him … it's embarrassing."

"Dick." I didn't know what to say. I tried to remember what I'd thought when I'd first met him. I'm sure I didn't swoon. What I remembered most about that first class was being scared and excited. I told myself I wanted to know how to write a detective in case I found another dead body. But I think secretly, way down, I wanted to try to write. Listening to Dick had calmed my fears and made me hope that maybe I could do it.

"So, tell me," I said.

"I met Mellie that day I came to the studio with you. You were talking to Sean when she came over and asked me about her character. She knew I'd worked with you on the script and thought I might have some insights. Sean called her back to the set, and she suggested we meet for drinks later. I was flattered."

"And did you two meet?" I asked.

"Yes. We talked about *Steamed*, about your writing, about my writing, about her acting. She wasn't like she was later. She was charming that first night. Funny. And we met again for dinner a few times. The second time, I told her I was working on a new idea for a series. *Cereal Killer.* A ten epi-sode drama about a husband and wife detective team who's tracking a female serial killer who's a—"

"Mom." Dick and I had talked about this project. He'd told me that he'd based the female detective on me, in a loose sort of way.

"I thought it was a very different drama...seeing work-ing parents looking for someone who is a good parent, even though they're a despicable person."

"And?"

"Mellie really wanted the role of the killer. She didn't come right out and say it, but hindsight is twenty-twenty, you know. I thought she really liked me." He shrugged, as if the fact that she used him didn't hurt, but I could see that it had.

I reached out and took his hand in mine. "You had an affair?"

"Yes. It lasted a month. One morning, we were having breakfast when a friend called. I didn't pick up, but she left a message."

"Another girlfriend?" I asked.

"No. An actress friend. She said she'd couldn't wait to read the script and to call her."

"*Cereal Killer?*"

He nodded. "Kristin mentioned she was tired of playing the girl next door. She wanted the killer mom's role."

"And that's when…?" I prompted.

He twirled his coffee cup, staring at it so he didn't have to meet my eyes. "Mellie laughed," he said quietly, "and said she was sorry my friend was going to be disappointed that I'd already found my killer mom."

"Oh."

"I know. I realized she was just using me to get the part. If I was dating her, if I wrote the role for her and said as much to the producers, she figured she'd have the part."

"And…?"

"I thought about breaking up with her right then," Dick said. "But I was sort of in shock. I guess she was a good actress because I'd bought that she cared for me. Despite the fact I am who I am. I called her later that night and said I was sorry that things weren't working out for us, and I thought it would be best if we ended things now, on a friendly basis."

Suddenly the scene Honey had described made sense. "Mellie doesn't do friendly breakups?"

"No. She found me at a restaurant the next day, upended a drink on me, and told me the only way I got to break up with her was over her dead body."

"You couldn't have been afraid that if you told me that I'd have thought you'd done it?" I said.

"No. It's not in your nature to distrust your friends. When you love its wholeheartedly, Quincy. I knew you'd believe me. And I planned to tell you. But not while Cal was sitting there. And not because I thought that he wouldn't believe me, but because I was pretty sure he wouldn't have a clue what it's like being a guy like me."

"Dick." My heart broke for my friend.

He was still staring at the coffee. "I work in a town of beautiful people. I am not beautiful."

I still felt bad for him, but he didn't need my sympathy. He needed a kick in the butt. "Seriously, Dick? I've had three kids. I have a baby-pooch, even though all the boys are in their twenties. If I haven't lost it by now, what are the odds I ever will? I'm average in a town of above-average people. So are you. It plays with your mind, skews your view of yourself. But you and me? We're normal. Neither of us is the most beautiful person in any given room, but our mother's didn't have to tie porkchops around our necks in order to get the dog to play with us."

He laughed at that.

"Mellie was awful," I said. "She used you. But it had nothing to do with you…it was her."

I live in a town where beauty counts. But maybe my family had prepared me for it. With them, brains and a degree counted. Somewhere along the line I'd realized I'd never be the most beautiful, and I'd never be the smartest. I was me. And ninety-nine percent of the time, I was totally okay with that.

"So, that's it?" I asked him after I'd sat back down. "There's nothing else you're not telling me?"

"Nothing."

"And what you told me from the party?"

He held up his right hand. 'The God's honest truth. I got drunk, but the reason was that Mellie had showed up. She looked through me, as if I were invisible. Then she threw herself at Jonas. And for one moment, as she wrapped herself around him, she did look at me. It was a *this-is-the-kind-of-man-I-belong-with* sort of look. So I started drinking."

"And you heard someone fight?"

"I was only half awake and drunk. I thought it was Lady Gaga and Pink—that it was just a dream. But I've been thinking about it since. I think there's a chance that Pink was Mellie. I had a dream afterward and Mellie was singing to me while hanging on ribbons, like Pink did for that one award show? I think it got all mixed up in my head. Anyway, I don't doubt she made a play for someone else. Mellie was a woman who couldn't be without a man for long. And she preferred men who could further her career."

"Jonas can further her career?"

"He is an established actor," Dick said. "Not the kind of guy who normally does made-for-TV movies. If she was paired with him it would definitely increase her exposure."

That's why Shia wanted him as well. I felt sorry for Jonas.

"If she was fighting with someone it was probably Shia,." Dick said, as if he'd read my mind. "Shia was Jonas's date. Did she say anything about fighting with Mellie?"

"No," I said.

"It might be nothing," Dick said. "Sometimes people don't tell you things that they feel will paint them in a bad light."

"Sometimes people are stupid and don't realize that in a true friend's eyes, the light's never bad." I reached across the Formica table and put my hand on his. "Dick, if you showed up in the middle of the night and told me there was a dead body in your trunk, I wouldn't ask questions. I'd just go get the shovel."

He laughed at that, then ever-the-writer said, "I'm going to incorporate that into *Cereal Killers.*"

I laughed, too, and we started tossing around ideas for his new project.

But even as we did, I was thinking about Mellie, Shia, and Jonas.

I needed to go talk to Shia again.

I was tempted to stop on my way home. Shia lived in the neighborhood. But I felt as if I'd already violated Cal's trust enough, so I went home.

He wasn't there.

But he'd left a note on the counter. *"Went home to get a few things. If I don't beat you back, I should be there shortly. Love you."*

I smiled. I don't think the boys ever left me notes anymore. They just texted me. And that's how I'd have left Cal a note as well, with a text.

But there was something more personal about a note scratched on the back of a deposit slip. I traced his last two words and sat down on the couch to wait for him.

When he came home, I'd tell him everything about my conversation with Dick.

And then we'd both go see Shia. I didn't think there was any way that Shia could have strangled Mellie.

But what about her father? I moved both their photos to the center of the white-board and then moved Jonas and Mellie's, too.

Shia was Jonas's date to the Morties. He was an established actor who lent her an air of legitimacy as she tried to escape her reality star roots. She was sweeter than Mellie, but she was willing to use people to get where she wanted to go.

Mellie would have wanted Jonas for much the same reason. She'd been in the business for years, but hadn't really advanced beyond supporting roles. It wasn't really her talent holding her back but her personality.

Jonas had nothing to gain from either woman. But a star always had something to lose. What if Mellie knew something about him and was blackmailing him? Could he be threatened enough to kill her?

And finally, Shia's father. He admittedly gave her everything she was wanted. What if Shia wanted Jonas and Mellie was in the way?

I called Cal. "Hey," he said when he picked up.

I could tell from the background noise he had me on the car's speaker.

"I'm home. Are you on your way?"

"I want to stop at the station on my way back, if you don't mind."

"No. I have something I need to tell you."

"About Mellie?"

"Yes. I think the pieces are starting to make sense. At least enough sense to warrant us going back to talk to a few people."

"Like?" he asked.

"Shia and her dad."

"What led you to that?"

"I'll walk you through it when you get home. I'll just sit here and mull a bit longer while I wait for you."

"Okay," he said. "I'll give your *Detective Charlie* a call and see if he wants to stop in, too."

"That's a good idea. Have you called him Charlie to his face? I'm not sure he's fond of it."

"He's not," Cal said.

"Which means you're going to call him that all the time?"

He laughed. "Probably. It has a better ring to it than Randolph."

"Hey, when this is over, I want a do-over." I hadn't known I was going to say the words until I did.

"A do-over of what?" Cal asked.

I started to tell him, but I decided I'd surprise him. I'd think of something totally romantic and re-propose.

"I'll tell you later."

"If we want to do-over what we did last night, I'm in."

I laughed and hung up before he could make some other sexually charged retort.

I didn't want to be hot and bothered. I wanted to figure this out. So, I went back to staring at the white-board.

I looked at all the pictures. Given that Mellie was strangled, I was pretty sure most of the women were in the clear.

I didn't think any of the men in my family had a motive. Even if Mellie had hit on them, they'd have brushed her aside. Macs were loyal to a fault.

My eyes kept darting to Jonas, Shia, and her father.

I think it was Jonas. Yeah, it was a gut feeling. And while I know that's not enough to base an investigation on for a real cop, I wasn't a real cop, so I could keep him in mind, but look beyond him.

I didn't think Shia could manage it.

But what about her dad? He was big. He worked as a security specialist. And he'd even admitted to giving her everything she wanted.

I pulled out my laptop and Googled him. Dubrinski Security was the first link that popped up. I opened it. There was no picture, which I guess made sense if you did security. You wouldn't want your picture out and about. But his bio was there.

The doorbell rang as I clicked the link. Reluctantly, I left my laptop and opened the door…to find Shia's father glaring at me.

"Mr. Dubrinski," I started, but I didn't get any further. He pushed past me and stalked into my house.

"Sir, what are you doing?" I asked.

"Where's your white-board. Don't deny you have one," he warned, "because you do. Everyone in the world knows you do now."

He walked into the living room and stared at the two boards.

Then he walked over to the laptop, swished across the mouse pad and woke it up. There was his firm's information.

He looked from the computer to the white-board, then back again before turning around and looking at me. "So you know."

"I don't know anything." Now, a smart person might try to deny it, but having seen his picture in the center of the white-board and then my computer, I didn't think all the denials in the world would do any good. I took a deep breath, weighed my next words, and finally said, "I don't know, but *we* suspect. Unfortunately, suspecting and proving are two very different things."

I put my hand in my back pocket and clicked the phone button, then Cal's speed dial. At least I hoped it was Cal's speed dial. If it wasn't, I was hoping whoever it was I did call would realize what was going on and call Cal or the cops... someone.

"*We?*" he asked, catching my deliberate word choice.

"Do you really think my fiancé—a cop—would let me investigate another murder on my own? We're working together on this one. He came to your house with me because he's not letting me out of his sight."

I immediately saw the flaw in that argument.

"Yeah, so where is he?"

"He's on his way. He went to get Detective Randolph and then we were coming to see you, so thank you, Mr. Dubrinski. You saved us a trip."

"You're lying," he said and took an ominous step in my direction.

Everything in me wanted to take a step back and maintain some distance between us, but I held my ground. I might have taken Mr. Banning's killer on my own, but Mr. Dubrinski was a brick house. I might get in one lucky kick to his nether region, but I suspect I'd only get one chance and it wouldn't stop him for long.

I prayed that Cal was hearing this, that I dialed right, that he was coming with Detective Charlie and saving the day.

"Why couldn't you just leave it alone?" he asked.

I'd already proved I could rescue myself if needs be, but I wasn't stupid enough to think I could *always* rescue myself—that I'd never need assistance. And I knew this was one of those times I needed all the help I could get.

My best bet was to keep Mr. Dubrinski talking as long as possible.

"I didn't want to investigate this at all, but everyone I loved was at that party. How could I not step in? I know you love Shia. I could see that at the house. So I know you understand."

"It's always been her and me," he said softly, "ever since her mother ran out. Do you know how hard it is on a kid to lose a parent?"

"No. My husband and I divorced, but he was always there for the boys. Still, I do know what it's like to feel like a single parent. As if whatever you do can never be enough to make up for the fact they didn't get to grow up in an all-American, two-parent household."

"Sheila was so beautiful," he said. "So talented. She deserved everything she wanted."

"And you loved her so much you tried to help her." I nodded and gave him what I hoped was an understanding look.

"I put the addition on the garage so she could have her own space while she was breaking into the business. Then she got cast in *LA Shore*. They made her look like. ..." He let the sentence die.

He didn't need to finish. I knew exactly what *LA Shore* made her look like. She'd hopped from man to man, from bed to bed in the show.

I couldn't imagine how hard that had to have been for her father to watch.

"After it was over, she had offers. But not for the kind of shows a father wants his daughter to do. I was working for Benet Margin and convinced him to take a look at Sheila. He did and she was in *Casting Callers*, determined to use it to springboard to real acting gigs."

"Did she know that you asked Mr. Margin to look at her?" I asked.

Mr. Dubrinski gave me an are-you-crazy sort of look. I wanted to say, *no, I'm not crazy, you are*, but thought it was best to keep that particular opinion to myself.

"I've helped her wherever, whenever I can, but I've never told her about any of it," he said.

"You're a good father."

"But I didn't mean for this to happen." He gestured to the white-board.

I didn't want to ask what had happened. If he confessed, then he might think it would be best if I was out of the picture.

But now that he had started, he didn't need any prompting.

He said, "I went to your party to have a drink with Sheila. To tell her how proud I was that she'd done such a good job with Tiny. She should have won a Mortie, you know? But even without that, for a first legit acting gig, she'd done a great job. And then I saw that guy Sheila liked talking to that Mellie woman. Sheila said Mellie had been hitting on Jonas since she'd crashed your party. He was Sheila's date, you know. I work with Hollywood types all the time. So I figured that since Mellie had crashed, I'd do you a favor and ask her to leave. I saw her heading upstairs, and I followed."

I wanted to beg him not to say more, but I was pretty sure that Cal and Charlie wanted to hear the rest, so I didn't say anything. I didn't try to stop him.

"I followed her into a bedroom. '*No one wants you here, it's time to go,*' I said.

"She looked at me and sneered. '*Quincy sent the hired help to throw me out? Or was it Peri? Either way, I'm not leaving.*'

" '*No one sent me,*' I told her. '*You're not important enough for anyone to worry about. But you're making a fool of yourself. It would be best if you left, and better yet, if you stopped throwing yourself at every man in the place. No one wants you. Everyone was relieved you were cast as a one-movie character. When* Dusted *gets picked up, the cast will be back without you.*'"

"I'm sure that didn't go over well," I said.

"It didn't. Mellie screeched and launched herself at me. I grabbed her when she came in reach and threw her on the bed."

"And then?"

"She hit her head on the headboard and for a moment, I thought that had knocked some sense into her, but she got back up and came at me again, so I tossed her back on the bed, harder this time. She hit the wall, then the headboard that time. And she started to scream. I told her to shut up, but she wound up to scream again and ... I just wanted her to be quiet and listen to reason. There was no reason for her to be at the party, trying to steal Sheila's guy. I told her to stop fighting, to stay still and be quiet. But she hit me, and clawed at me. And then she didn't any more."

He shuddered. "It was an accident. Self-defense. I never meant for her to die. I tried giving her mouth to mouth, but it didn't help."

Yeah, I wasn't a doctor, but I was pretty sure there wasn't any coming back from a crushed throat.

"I'm sure the DA will understand when you tell him, Mr. Dubrinski," I said softly.

His expression had me wishing I'd stayed silent.

"Tell him?" he asked.

In for a penny, in for a pound. "When you confess. The cops and the district attorney will definitely understand. I mean, Cal met Mellie. He knows what she was like. That she was attacking you. You were just defending yourself."

He shook his head. "They'll never buy it."

"It's the truth."

"This is Hollywood," he said. "The truth doesn't matter. The only thing that matters is the story. And the story plays out much better if I'm a crazy father who is intent on giving his daughter everything, even if it means killing her competition. Hell, I'm sure they'll spin it so that Mellie and Sheila were up for the same part and I took out my daughter's competition."

He took another step toward me.

I still held my ground. If I ran, he might try and catch me, and by *try* I mean there was no way Mr. Buff-and-Strong-Like-an-Ox wouldn't catch me and toss me around like a rag doll, too.

"This is a mess," he said. He stopped, not coming any closer. He looked as if he was running through his options.

I only saw two for him. Kill me and shut me up or confess.

I knew which option I was hoping for.

"It is a mess," I said. "But you know what we have to do. Why don't you call Cal on your phone—I'll give you his number. Tell him you're turning yourself in. If you do that, you control the story. You're right, this is Hollywood and it's all about the story. But the real story is compelling, too. Mellie was awful. Everyone hated her. She wasn't up for the same role as Shia, because anyone who met them would always rather work with Shia than Mellie. You were being thoughtful, trying to make sure an uninvited guest left a party. That's your job. You've done the same thing for a client countless times. You couldn't have known that Mellie would fly into a rage and attack you. You were defending yourself and things...got out of hand."

By *out of hand*, I meant his hands wrapped around her neck and squeezed until she was dead.

I continued, "It wasn't intentional or premeditated. I'm sure the DA will give you some kind of deal. Because if he had to put you on trial, all of Mellie's hatefulness would come out. If they call me to the stand, I'll tell them that I didn't like her. She was a mean woman. She even made a play for my fiancé."

He pulled out his phone. "Give me his number."

He sank to the couch as if he didn't have the energy left to even stand. I sat in the chair across the room from him because while I didn't think he was going to do me in, I wasn't dumb enough to take any chances.

Well, any *more* chances.

He dialed. "Detective Parker. This is Miller Dubrinski— Shelia, Shia's father. I'm at Quincy's house and I'd like to confess to murdering Mellie Anderson. Could you bring the detective in charge of the case and meet me here?"

He nodded. "She's fine." He paused. "Okay." He clicked off the phone. "They'll be here in a minute."

I nodded.

He stared at the white-board a moment, then said, "I'm not going to hurt you."

"Uh, thank you."

He nodded. "I want to ask you something and I don't have any right to ask you. But no matter what, I'm doing time for this. I'll set up everything so Sheila can live in the house and be taken care of. But I won't be able to watch out for her. Like I said, I don't have any right to ask, but you're a single mom. You get it."

I didn't need him to go on. "I'll watch out for her."

"Maybe have her over at holidays if she'll come? She won't have anyone when I'm locked away."

"I will," I promised.

He nodded. "I thought you would. I've seen how close you are with your ex-husband's wife. I figured you could ignore the fact that Sheila has a murderer for a father and simply see the sweet kid who's all alone."

I got up and moved from me chair to the couch next to Mr. Dubrinski. "I'll treat her like she's one of my own. She'll be one of the family."

"I saw your family at the party. And not just your folks and brothers, but all the people there. You love them all, and they'd do anything for you. Sheila could use people like that in her life. Thank you."

I nodded and at that moment, the door burst open and Cal and Detective Charlie raced into the living room with guns drawn.

"You can put those away, guys. Mr. Dubrinski is turning himself in and willing to make a confession. Right?"

"Right," he said softly.

"I'm going to leave you guys here and just ask that you give me an hour to go find Shia before you take him in and book him. I don't want her to hear this on the news."

"Quince," Cal started, as if he planned on lecturing me. I gave him a pleading look and he looked at Charlie, then back at me. "One hour. After that, we're putting him in the car and taking him to the station."

"Fine."

I patted Mr. Dubrinski's shoulder and hurried out the door.

I called Shia's phone. "Hello?" she said.

"Shia it's Quincy. I have some news."

"Is it *Dusted?* Oh, Quincy, I just knew they'd pick it up."

My heart broke because she was expecting good news and I was going to bring her news that would shatter her world. "Are you at home?"

"Yeah."

"Wait for me there," I said.

I'd meant what I told Mr. Dubrinski. I would watch over Shia for him.

I wish I felt better about solving this mystery, but I couldn't quite manage it.

CHAPTER TEN

THE NEXT WEEK, we heard that *Dusted* had been picked up. The exposure from our Mortie's and Mellie's murder didn't hurt.

This was Hollywood and the story was everything.

I was asked more than once if I was planning to write the screenplay for Mellie's murder. I gave the same answer every time—an emphatic no.

I was working on a new idea. *My Next Ex* about a woman who was looking for love, and rather than finding it, she found a bunch of ex's who became her best friends. So she gave up and rather than looking for the love of her life, she was looking for a man who could be her next ex and fit into her band of friends who were former boyfriends.

It was light and funny.

And there's not a murder anywhere in the mix.

Two weeks after Mr. Dubrinski was arrested, I called Cal and asked him to meet me at Big G's.

I was talking to Big G when Cal, my fiancé, walked in.

"You gonna sit with us?" he asked his friend and headed for a table.

I snagged his hand and said, "No, not here," and then led him to the office in the back.

Big G didn't follow.

There were salads on the desk.

"This is where we had our first official date," I said.

"That wasn't a date," Cal said. "It was an interrogation. I simply fed you because I was afraid you were going to pass out if I didn't."

"You brought me to your friend's place and fed me because it was a date … you just didn't realize it yet." I nodded at a chair and he sat down.

He looked at me. "So what is this all about?"

I slid the engagement ring off my finger and handed it to him.

"Quincy, no," Cal said. "Whatever this is, we'll work it out. I—"

"Shh," I said as I sank to my knees. "It's been pointed out that after not saying yes to your very romantic Christmas proposal and making you wait so long in engagement limbo, I owed you a better proposal than in a hall outside a murder scene."

Cal realized what was going on and grinned. "Honey, you finally said yes … that was pretty much perfect in my book."

"Still let me try and do better." There on my knee, I asked, "Caleb Parker, will you marry me?"

He pulled me up and onto his lap. "Yes."

He slid the ring on my finger. "I just have one request."

"Love you forever?" I guessed. "It's done."

"Two requests. Love me forever, and no more *Quincy Mac, Amateur PI.*"

"Done and done," I promised and I meant it. Well, unless someone in my family needed me. Or …

Well, I meant it until I didn't.

But the loving him forever? There was no question about that.

Bonus Chapter: The Wedding

"**Q**UINCY MAC YOU ARE absolutely stunning." Tiny's voice was all breathless wonder.

I'd been having feelings of deja vu for the last two weeks. This one was particularly strong.

Tiny had said those exact words to me as I stood wearing a pumpkin colored bridesmaid dress for her wedding. This time, I was the one in a wedding dress and Tiny once again had full-blown wedding-fever. And again, everything she said was breathless.

Breathless wonder.

Breathless excitement.

Breathless anticipation.

Just like for her own wedding.

"Breathe, Tiny," I reminded helpfully as I had countless times the last few weeks.

"You look so. ..." She started to cry.

Breathless and crying. Those seemed to be her go-to emotions for any wedding.

"... so beautiful," Tiny finally managed. The rest of the women gathered in my bedroom, echoed their agreement.

When I'd been wearing that pumpkin color bridesmaid dress, I'd lied and told Tiny I loved it. The truth was, I loved her and if having me look like a walking jack 'o lantern made her happy, then I'd been prepared to be the happiest jack o' lantern ever.

Today I didn't necessarily feel beautiful—I could pull off cute on a good day, but beautiful was a bit much to expect. But I did feel good. I was wearing a simple white linen skirt and jacket, with the smallest hint of the Mclean plaid as an accent at the sleeves and jacket closure.

"It's almost time," she said.

Despite the fact Mom, Tiny, and Peri had wanted a full-blown wedding, I wanted something smaller. And Cal stood by me. Peri had offered to host it at her house, but after Mellie's murder, I'll confess, I didn't even feel slightly tempted. Instead we were having it in my backyard. Now people from other regions might have to worry that a backyard wedding was an iffy thing without tents for backup. But this is California… the odds were in my favor, I'd maintained.

I woke up to the sun streaming through my window.

I thought it was a good omen.

But seriously, as long as we didn't find a dead body, I didn't care what the weather was like. I was marrying Cal.

June is a traditional wedding month, and that worked for me because all three boys were home from college for summer break. It also worked because I couldn't wait any longer than that to marry Cal.

I marveled that I'd once thought I could make it to August before we were officially engaged.

"It's time," Tiny said.

I was beset by a flurry of hugging. Peri, Honey, my sisters-in-law, and even Theresa hugged me. They all left the room, which left just me, Tiny and my mom.

My mom said, "Honey, I have two things to say, one is thank you for letting me plan this wedding with you. I'm finally wearing a mother-of-the-bride's dress. Mother-of-the-groom isn't nearly as much fun, though don't tell your brothers that I said that. And secondly, I want to offer you a bit of motherly advice."

"Don't go to bed angry?" I teased.

"No. That's bound to happen. I'm not even going to pass on my mother's advice." She chuckled in such a way that I really wanted to know what that was.

"Which was?"

"Never tell a man no … it only takes a couple minutes."

The three of us burst out laughing.

"Not if you're doing it right," Tiny managed to spit out.

When our laughter died down, Mom said, "Love Cal. Love him enough to forgive him if you do go to bed angry. Love him, laugh with him and have a happy life. You've said that I was disappointed you didn't become a doctor, but Quincy, that wasn't my greatest wish for you. My greatest wish has always been that you be happy … and that you live up to your potential. It's a wonderful thing when a mother can see her wishes for her child has come true."

I felt myself tear up.

"No," Tiny bellowed. "No crying. The two of you will mess your makeup. Judith, go take your seat. I'll bring Quincy out in a second."

Mom kissed my cheek and scurried. Tiny the wedding-enforcer was scary enough to make Judith Quincy Mac run.

"And you," she said. "Your mother's right. Love him. And let him love you. You deserve nothing but a life of love and happiness."

And with that, Tiny led me to through the house to the sliding glass door that led to my backyard. There, Hunter, Miles, Eli and my father all waited to escort me down the aisle.

Hey, I'm a feminist and I'm not saying I believe any man has the right to *give me away* to someone, but these four men meant the world to me and I was happy they were walking down with me.

And there, at the end of our makeshift aisle between the folding chairs I'd borrowed from Jerome's newest set, was Cal...wearing a kilt of Mclean plaid, just like the boys and Dad. Everyone stood as I entered. And every male there, from Big G to Dick was wearing a kilt. Jerome was, too. From his expression I knew that Peri had forced him.

Then I spotted Detective Charlie...also in a kilt.

No one had warned me about the wedding's dress code. I laughed as I saw all the knobby, knocky kneed men in my life. Then I teared up again.

Tiny turned around and gave me a thumbs up. I knew she and my mom had planned this.

I shot them both a look filled with love.

Speaking of love—I walked toward the man I loved. A man I'd met at one murder scene and had become officially engaged to at another.

The man who drove me crazy and made me laugh.

The man I could envision growing old with.

The ceremony went along in a very traditional manner, until the minister told me to repeat after him.

"I Quincy take you, Caleb...."

"I Quincy," I parroted. "Take you, Caleb."

"To be my wedded husband. To have and to hold, from this day forward...."

"To be my wedded husband." I wasn't sure after Jerome I'd ever marry again. But I couldn't imagine going another day without being married to Cal. "To have and to hold, from this day forward."

"…for better, for worse.…"

"For better for worse," I said. Being with Cal made me a better person, and he'd shown me in so many ways that he'd stand by me no matter what. With the boys, with my family, with whatever life threw at me."

"…for richer, for poorer, in sickness and in health, to love and to cherish, 'till death do us part," the minister said.

"For richer, for poorer, in sickness and in health, to love and to cherish, 'till death do us part," I could promise him these things wholeheartedly.

"*AND.*…" The minister grinned as he drew out the word and said it with such emphasis that I knew something was up. I glanced at Cal who had a very-pleased-with-himself expression on his face.

"I pledge," the minister continued, "that if I'm ever investigating a crime, I'll let you be my partner in that, too."

I burst out laughing, and when I had myself under control, I repeated the words.

I hadn't thought to add anything to our very traditional vows, but I didn't need to make Cal promise anything else. I knew that whatever happened, he'd be there, right beside me no matter what. And when you know something like that about someone, you don't need any other promises.

The day was a blur of Mclean tartan and happiness. I danced, I ate, I laughed, and I teared up…but only happy tears.

And when the party ended, I sat next to my kilt-wearing husband and whispered, "I love you."

"I love you, too," he whispered back.

And that's why I can end this story with a very decisive promise.

They lived happily ever after...
at least until...

Thank you for reading Swept Up: A Maid in LA Mystery! *I hope you enjoyed it. If you did, please help other readers find this book by writing a review.*

A lot of readers have asked for more Quincy Mac stories. I've been mulling a fifth book. If you want to be sure to hear about it, you can visit HollyJacobs.com and sign up for my newsletter!

In case you missed the first three books, they're:
Book #1 Steamed: A Maid in LA Mystery
Book#2 Dusted: A Maid in LA Mystery
Book #3 Spruced Up: A Maid in LA Holiday Novella

2–1–2014
Dear Reader,

And thus ends Quincy's adventures. Well, maybe. I wanted to leave the possibility of a fifth story open. But in case this was the last, I tried to make sure she had a happily-ever-after. When we first met Quincy, she was a once-wanna-be-actress who'd become a harried business owner and a single mom. As we finish this book, she's also a successful screenwriter and is married to the love of her life.

Because I often get reader letters asking about other characters in a story, I thought it would be fun to do a quick *"Where-Are-They-Now..."* ending for some of Quincy's friends.

Tiny had a baby boy. Salvador Addison Mardones Jr. Quincy called him Sal-Ad once and somehow that morphed into Caesar Salad, and finally to simply Caesar. The name will stick with him throughout his life. He'll never mind until he's older and falls in love with a woman named Cleo.

Jerome and Peri did divorce right on his schedule—but Peri's acting career had taken off and she met a very nice cowboy (well, an actor who was playing a cowboy on TV) named Buck and married him. She's still very good friends with Jerome and still the boys' favorite stepmother. Well, these days they don't call her that. You see, Quincy and Cal adopted her. They had Honey cater a lovely dinner where they presented her with her 'official' adoption papers. Quincy's entire family flew into LA for the party...they adopted her, too. When Peri married Buck, Cal walked her down the aisle and Quincy was her matron-of-honor. Peri's adoption papers hang in her living room. Her children call Quincy and Cal Grandma and Grandpa, despite the fact they claim they are way too young for those titles.

Big G still flirts with Quincy and swears he'll break her out of jail if needs be, but his wife, Honey, doesn't mind the flirting and says she'll be right there next him during the great jail break. These two foodies were meant for each other. (Cassandra and Julian are still together, too.)

Theresa is still the worst maid ever, but she's a fantastic manager of Mac'Cleaners' original store. Tiny and Quincy have Mac'Cleaner's franchises now and they are selling fast. Oh, and Theresa married Rob. They have a houseful of computer nerds. Theresa doesn't even clean her own house...she hired a Mac'Cleaner's maid.

Quincy's agent, Deanne, sold *Dusted* to the HeartMark Channel. And Sean, the director, was back again, and so was Shia as Tiny. Sean also directed Quincy's first major motion picture, *My Next Ex* and Peri starred in it. Quincy's collaborating with Dick on *Cereal Killers*. It's in its second season, and there's a lot of Mortie buzz. Shia's starring in it and comes to Quincy's for holidays... the family is thinking about another 'adoption.'

Dick has a new girlfriend. Her name is Pat. She's petite, feisty, and madly in love with him... which is good because he's planning to pop the question soon.

Detective Charlie moved to Cal's division and they became partners... and friends.

Oh, and the boys all graduated from college. Hunter's gone all Maccish and is in medical school. Miles is working with his father. And Eli... he's got his own show on Comedy Central. He's talking about getting a tattoo.

Now, in case you're thinking there couldn't be another story because I just told you what happened... there could. But since neither Quincy nor her author wanted her stumbling across dead bodies on a regular basis (or stumbling on art heists and forgeries), it would probably be a few years after *Swept Up*. I'll keep you posted.

But in the meantime, thank you so much for all your support for Quincy! I've been so very lucky to have you all in my corner. You've read my romantic comedies and my romance dramas. And now you've followed me to my cozy mysteries. Thank you all!

~Holly

BIO

Award-winning author Holly Jacobs has almost three million books in print worldwide. The first novel in her Everything But... series, *Everything But a Groom*, was named one of 2008's Best Romances by Booklist, and her books have been honored with many other accolades. She lives in Erie, Pennsylvania, with her husband and four children and two dogs, Ethel Merman and Ella Fitzgerald. You can visit her at http://www.HollyJacobs.com.

ALSO BY HOLLY JACOBS:

Romance+ Stories
Just One Thing
Same Time Next Summer
Her Second-Chance Family
Words of the Heart Series
Carry Her Heart
These Three Words
Hold Her Heart

Romantic Comedies
I Waxed My Legs for This?
A Day Late and a Bride Short
Bosom Buddies
Cinderella Wore Tennis Shoes

Cupid Falls
Christmas in Cupid Falls
A Simple Heart: A Cupid Falls Novella

Short Stories and Novellas
Able to Love Again
Labor Day
There He Was

13 Weeks
Nothing But Short Story Series:
Nothing But Love
Nothing But Heart
Nothing But Luck
Rather than buy them individually, try:
Short Stories for the Overworked and Under-Read Anthology

Maid in LA Series:
My first mystery series!!
Steamed: A Maid in LA Mystery
Dusted: A Maid in LA Mystery
Spruced Up: A Maid in LA Novella
Swept Up: A Maid in LA Mystery
All four books in one edition
Maid in LA Mysteries bundle

Perry Square Series:
Do You Hear What I Hear?
A Day Late and a Bride Short
Dad Today, Groom Tomorrow
Be My Baby
Once Upon a Princess
Once Upon a Prince
Once Upon a King
Here With Me

Everything But... Series:
Everything But a Groom
Everything But a Bride
Everything But a Wedding

Everything But a Christmas Eve
Everything But a Mother
Everything But a Dog

WLVH Series:
Pickup Lines
Lovehandles
Night Calls
Laugh Lines

Whedon Series:
Unexpected Gifts
A One-of-a-Kind Family
Homecoming Day
A Father's Name

Valley Ridge Series:
You Are Invited… *A Valley Ridge Wedding*
April Showers, *A Valley Ridge Wedding*
A Walk Down the Aisle, *A Valley Ridge Wedding*
A Valley Ridge Christmas

Did you miss Quincy's first adventure,
Steamed: A Maid in LA Mystery?
She based her Mortie Award winning screenplay on it!
Find out what happened to Mr. Banning and who dunnit!
Here's the excerpt:

When I moved to LA, I was an eighteen year old with stars in my eyes. Well, not exactly in my eyes, but rather *on* my eyes. My high school best friend bought me sunglasses with lenses shaped like stars for when I *Made It*. Lottie always said the words in such a way you just knew they were capitalized.

Made It.

Yes, I graduated from high school and moved to LA. I planned to be a famous actress. Lottie made me promise I'd wear my star-shaped glasses on my first Oscar red carpet walk. My goal was to take Hollywood by storm.

These days, those glasses are in a drawer in my bedroom and I have two much smaller goals. One is that I want to wear my jeans without a muffin-top. After three kids, I'd developed a bit of a baby-pooch that wants to creep out above the waistband of my jeans. I longed for the days when pants had waistbands that were higher. Back then you could tuck your baby-pooch in. These days your options are exercise, wear Spanx, or learn to suck it in.

I tend to suck it in…when I remember.

My second goal is an empty nest.

It's not that I don't love my boys. I do. I have three sons—Hunter, Miles and Eli. They are eighteen, seventeen and sixteen. I've been a parent practically my entire adult life. I'm ready for a time when I simply have to worry about me and no one else.

This summer is my trial empty-nest.

The boys left last night to spend four weeks in the Bahamas with their father and his most recent wife, Peri.

Now, my place isn't exactly a dump, but compared to their dad's house, my three bedroom bungalow in the out-of-the-way neighborhood of Van George is a cardboard box in some alley.

And while thirty-eight isn't exactly over-the-hill, next to Peri, the twenty-year-old, I am ancient.

I miss my boys (and I realize the irony in longing for an empty nest, but missing them when they're on vacation). I try not to mind when my ex takes the boys on fabulous vacations—and most of the time I don't mind—but getting ready for work in a quiet house, I minded.

My ex, movie producer Jerome Smith, is a nice guy…a nice guy with a taste for younger women. Specifically women between the ages of twenty and twenty-five. The exact ages I married, then divorced him. Or rather, he divorced me.

Jerome had two marriages before me, and three marriages since, all within those same parameters. His current wife's my favorite. I really like Peri despite the way her breasts perk and mine just sort of… well, hang loosely if they're not strapped down. I think Peri sort of appeals to my maternal instincts. I don't have a daughter.

Maybe I'll adopt her when Jerome divorces her.

TGIF, I told myself. I'm thirty-eight, and until the boys come home from their summer visit with their father, I'm footloose and fancy-free.

Maybe it isn't exactly the life I'd dreamed of when I moved to LA, but it's a good life.

Oh, sometimes I still wish that I was starring in some movie of the week instead of heading into Mac'Cleaners.

Yes, that's right—I no longer have stars in or on my eyes. Rather than achieving stardom, I have three sons and clean houses for a living. It's honest work, and it's flexible enough that when I was younger I could take time off and go on auditions. Now that I'm part owner and thirty-eight, I don't go to many auditions.

Okay, so I haven't been on an audition in five years— I've discovered that I'm a size twelve girl in a size two world.

I missed the fame and fortune boat.

Okay, so I could live without fame or fortune, if only I could figure out what I wanted to do with my life sometime before menopause hit. Owning a business keeps the boys and me afloat financially but lately, I'd had a feeling that it was time for a change. The kids weren't such kids anymore. Hunter would start college in the fall.

That empty nest is just around the bend. Soon I'll be able to live my own life.

And I know I want something more.

I'd said I wanted to act since I was six. I never gave any thought to doing something else. But it's clear that acting isn't going to be my ultimate career.

So while I wait to figure out what I want to do, I clean houses. I need to figure out soon because I'll be turning forty in a couple years. Forty sounds so very grown up, and grown-ups should have some idea about the direction they want their lives to take.

But I wasn't going to think about direction today.

Today, I was going to get my work done and then go do something decadent.

I'd like to say I was planning to go to a bar and pick up guys—well at least pick up a guy—but I'll probably end up going to the store and picking up Ben and Jerry's, then head home and try and catch up on all the chick-flicks the boys make me miss.

Feeling a bit better, I walked into the small brick storefront that was only a mile from my house. It proudly proclaimed Mac'Cleaners on the plate glass window with a tartan weaving through the letters. I walked through the small reception room and back to my partner, Tiny's office.

Big mistake.

There's nothing worse than starting the day as a single, directionless, mother of three and then walking into the middle of the wonderful world of weddings.

Tiny's marrying Salvador Mardones in September. September 30th to be exact. And she's going slightly insane ... a bit further over the brink each day.

"Tiny?" I called, hoping she was somewhere in the sea of tulle and satin.

"I'm here, Quincy," she said from the back corner.

Tiny's not very…tiny that is. She's five eight and looks like a model. Skin the color of strong tea and dark hair with a tendency to curl. She's gorgeous and simply a beautiful soul. We make an interesting pair, what with me having Irish fair skin, a light sprinkling of freckles that might have been cute when I was in my teens, but aren't as much when at thirty-eight. And my hair…well, it was blond when I moved to LA thanks to Lottie and Miss Clairol. These days, it has gone back to its brownish roots…literally.

Tiny smiled as I walked in, and I couldn't muster up true annoyance that her smile was messing with my grouchy mood because she radiated happiness. The kind of happiness I knew she deserved.

"It's getting worse, isn't it?" she asked, gesturing at her office.

I surveyed the room. "Yeah."

"I just can't help myself. I want this wedding to be perfect because Sal's perfect."

Truth is, Sal is perfect. He's my five five height, balding and has a beer belly that makes my small baby-pooched stomach look like washboard abs.

But he's truly one of the nicest guys in the world.

Tiny had a history of dating losers. But that was over because Sal…well, he's a winner.

"The wedding will be perfect," I promised.

I'd see to it, even though I'd rather have wisdom teeth pulled than plan a wedding this elegant.

Me, if I ever get married again, I'm eloping. Something fast and simple. Someone saying the official words, then me and my new husband back at some hotel having sex. Lots and lots of sex.

It had been a while, which might explain why my mind skipped right over finding Mr. Right and a wedding and went right to the sex.

"Speaking of help," Tiny said slowly, "we need some today. Theresa's out."

Rats.

"It's my turn, isn't it?" I asked, though I knew the answer.

She nodded.

When one of our employees calls in sick, we take turns filling in.

Today it was my turn to fill in.

I should have just gone back to bed this morning.

Grumbling to myself, I left Tiny to hold down the fort and took Theresa's folder for the day. The nice thing about working outside the office is that the day always went fast.

Today was no exception. By three in the afternoon, I was on my way to the last job.

As soon as I finished Mr. Banning's, I'd decided that I was going shopping for a new pair of shoes rather than Ben and Jerry's.

More money, less calories.

I thought the trade-off was worth it.

On a day like today, I didn't just want new shoes—I needed them. So, I grabbed Mr. Banning's printout from Theresa's folder. I was anxious to finish this last job.

Mr. Banning's was a BWP/wL.

A basic-weekly-pickup, with laundry.

I knocked on his door, even though the file said the odds of him being home at three o'clock in the afternoon were slim to nil.

I used our key and let myself in. I surveyed the living room with disgust. There was nothing basic about this job. The place was a mess.

I mean, a real pigsty. Worse than my boys' rooms…and that's saying something. Teenage boys are very toxic.

Mr. Banning was a whole new level of toxicity, though. Underwear was hanging from a chandelier, empty glasses and plates were scattered through the room.

Oh, geesh. Mr. Banning had a Mortie. All TV Network, ATVN, had begun to hand out the award ten years ago and it had quickly become one of the premier Hollywood awards.

Hey, I might not be an actual actress, but I know stuff.

I noticed not out of some sort of awe that I was cleaning a Mortie winner's home, but rather because the award was sitting in the middle of the leather couch, covered in something. Maybe someone had dipped it into some of the food. Ugh. It looked like they'd tried to wipe it off before throwing it on the couch, but they didn't wipe hard enough.

To top it off, there were footprints on the light beige carpet. Big footprints. Whoever wore those shoes had really big feet. Thankfully, there were only two. As if whoever made the prints realized they'd tracked in mud and took off their shoes, because those two prints were it.

Well, there'd been at least one considerate person.

I tried to make a mental list of how best to approach this job.

In the end, there was nothing to do but start. I gathered dishes and cups and the pots and pans in the kitchen and had the dishwasher running minutes later. I even hand-washed the Mortie—which was about as heavy as a bag of sugar, heavier than I'd thought the old-fashioned silver television would be—and gave it a thorough polish. When I was done, the inscription on the silver television screen really stood out. Steve Banning. *Dead Certain.*

I remembered that show. It was a comedy about a medical examiner's office.

I set the Mortie on the mantle, thinking that was a more appropriate place for it than the couch.

There was a desk next to the fireplace. It had an old relic of a computer on it. The keyboard's cord dangled over the edge of the desk. Yeah, that wasn't going to work well.

I plugged the keyboard into the back of the tower.

Next, I dragged a garbage can around the room and made short order of the rest of the mess.

I debated whether I should toss the chandelier's panties out, but opted to put them in the wash with a load of clothes. At least when Mr. Banning returned them to whoever they belonged to, they'd be clean.

Maybe they belonged to him?

The thought was enough to make me decide to concentrate on the job at hand rather than on the underclothing our Mortie-winning client wore.

There was a small steam-cleaner in the back of the Mac'Cleaners van. It made short work of the footprints. I worked on the laundry as I vacuumed and dusted. By then the dishwasher was finished, so I unloaded it then cleaned the kitchen.

I found the bra that matched the panties under the sink.

Personally, I didn't want to know why there was a bra under the sink. Maybe Mr. Banning had a dishwashing fetish and the mystery naked woman helped him out? The mental image was disturbing.

I knew walking into the place that Mr. Banning liked women.

It said so on his file. Right after BWP/wL it said *DOG.*

That's our code for he liked women a lot and liked a lot of them.

Yes, Mr. Banning is a dog…a letch.

But he never bothers the staff, so it didn't bother us.

Mac'Cleaners is an equal opportunity employee. We stake our reputation on good service and discretion.

This job was going to require a lot of discretion on my part. I wondered if Theresa's illness had anything to do with knowing that Mr. Banning's place was this bad and that she'd have to clean it up?

Kitchen done, I moved onto and finished the bathroom as well. Then I folded a load of laundry and put another one in the dryer. With the job almost done, I was getting excited about shoe shopping, which in LA is a unique treat. So many shoes, so few feet. I headed to Mr. Banning's bedroom.

If his living room was a pit, I really didn't want to know what condition his bedroom was in. Knowing that all that stood between me and some Santee Alley bargain shopping was this bedroom, I opened the door, took all of one step in and…screamed.

It wasn't a frustrated scream.

It wasn't even a this-guy-is-such-a-pig sort of scream.

No, it was more like a there's-a-bloody-dead-body-on-the-bed sort of scream.

Loud, long and more than a little crazed.

I wanted to keep screaming and run right out of the house, but I managed to get myself under control. The killer had to be long gone, or else he—or she—would have attacked me as I cleaned. I was safe. I couldn't say the same for poor Mr. Banning.

I reached in my back pocket, pulled out my cell phone and called 911.

"You've reached Los Angles emergency dispatch."

"I need help," I blurted out.

"What is the nature of your emergency?" the man on the other end of the phone asked.

"Mr. Banning's dead. There's blood on his head and his eyes are open."

Those eyes were going to give me nightmares for the rest of my life.

"Your address ma'am?"

"I'm at, he's at—" I had to think a moment, but then I somehow pulled his address from the fog that was my mind and blurted it out.

"Who are you?" the operator asked.

"I'm the maid. Quincy Mac."

Now, some people prefer the term domestic engineer, or some fancy title. I call it like I see it. I'm a maid.

I had no idea why I thought of what to call myself at that moment. Maybe it was nerves. After all it's not every day I find a dead client.

Thinking about my job description was easier than thinking about those eyes and all that blood.

"Ma'am are you sure he's dead?"

"I don't think there's any way someone could look that bloody and blue and still be breathing."

This was the ultimate topper to my day from hell.

A dead man in the bedroom.

As I talked to the operator, I walked outside. Not really walked, trotted. I moved fast. I mean, no way was I staying in a house with a dead guy.

I was thankful for my cell phone as I stepped out onto the bright sidewalk.

Perfect.

All that LA sunshine made it hard to believe that someone was dead a short distance away.

The emergency operator continued asking me questions. The company's name, my name and address, etc…

Personally, I sort of zoned out. I think I answered him all right but couldn't be sure.

Actually, I didn't want to be sure.

I just wanted to go home.

The police arrived, followed by an ambulance. They stopped and talked to me a minute, then hurried off to check on Mr. Banning.

I wondered how long I had to wait around.

I wanted to go home now.

I mean, I didn't even want to hunt for the perfect pair of bargain shoes or stop for Ben and Jerry's. That just shows how hard I'd been hit by this.

Anytime a woman passes up Ben and Jerry's or new shoes…well, it's moved beyond a bad day and turned into a found-a-dead-body-on-the-bed sort of day.

I was wondering if I could just sneak out. The authorities had my information already, so they didn't need me. But then *He* walked up to me.

He was tall, lean and oh-so-yummy. Dark hair with just a touch of grey at the temples.

Not one of LA's boy-toys who are a dime a dozen.

No, this was a real man walking toward me like some hero out of a movie.

Maybe he was here to take me away from all this.

Maybe he'd seen me from across the street looking fragile, yet still beautiful.

Okay, so beautiful was a bit unattainable. I'd settle for fragile and cute. Yeah, I could pull off cute on a good day and I felt very, very fragile at the moment.

Ah, my hero.

I sucked in my baby-pooch, pulled out my old acting class skills and concentrated on looking even more fragile and cute. It worked. He walked right up to me, shot me a concerned look, then … he flashed a badge.

I realized that his concerned look was more of an assessing look.

My hero was a cop.

Okay, so maybe *He* was a cop who was concerned because I looked so fragile?

"Ma'am? You're," he flipped open his little notepad in a very Adam-12 sort of way, and that particular mental-analogy really dated me I realized morosely as he finished, "Quincy Mac?"

"Yes." I thought about fluttering my eyelashes but decided to give up before I embarrassed myself.

"You're the one who found Mr. Banning and called 911?"

"Yes." I wanted to say more, so much more. But even a gorgeous knockout cop couldn't make me forget I'd just found a dead body, at least not for long. And thoughts of Mr. Banning, sitting on his bed, covered in blood with his eyes open, well, that sort of froze the words in my throat.

"The officer over there said that the house has been pretty much wiped clean."

I had professional pride in my job well done. "Not *pretty much*, all the way. Other than the bedroom, which I didn't clean for obvious reasons."

The cop quirked his eyebrow. "He said the bedroom was wiped clean as well."

I think the hunky cop just called me a liar.

Actually, I didn't just think it, I could see it in his eyes. The man actually thought I'd gone into a room with a dead body in it and cleaned it up?

My attraction to him slipped more than just a notch. It evaporated.

"Not by me," I assured him. "I took one look at the body on the bed, called 911 as I got the heck out of there. I guarantee that I didn't stop to clean the room first."

"But you admit you cleaned the rest of the house?" the cop asked.

"Of course I admit it. I'm the maid. That's what they pay me to do. Don't you think that if I'd have known someone had died, I'd have simply called the cops first? If you'd seen what a state the house was in when I arrived, you'd know I'd have welcomed an excuse not to clean it. But I did clean it and I did a fine job of it."

Cleaning houses is an honest profession. I might have been a bit befuddled, but even in my present state I wasn't going to let some cop make me feel less than the professional that I am.

He didn't answer my question. He simply asked, "And the other officers said there were footprints you steamed off the carpet?"

"Yes. I'm good at what I do. When Mac'Cleaners cleans a house, it's totally clean."

"Ma'am, the coroner says that Mr. Banning probably died sometime last night." He paused a moment and sort of gave me a hard stare with his charcoal grey eyes.

That stare did things to me ... my knees felt rather weak and my heart rate sped up. I don't think it was shock.

Lust.

That's what it felt like.

I hadn't had a good case of lust in a while. But I was pretty sure that I remembered how if felt and this was it.

"Quincy," he said, soft and low.

Yes, I wanted to say.

Oh, yes.

I've read that when someone experiences death they want to make love just to prove they're still alive, to prove that they can still feel something.

I think my lust for this cop went deeper than just a need to prove I was alive. It might have been a need to prove I still had a libido, but mainly I think it had something to do with a long, hard orgasm.

I was almost forty and I'd read enough magazine articles to know that meant I was reaching my sexual prime.

Only it had been a long time since I'd been primed.

This guy was making remember how much I enjoyed a good priming.

"Yes," I said out loud. Hoping he'd say, *let's forget about the dead body and get you home to bed.*

Oh, yeah. I wanted him to tuck me in, then tuck himself right next to me.

Naked.

"Quincy," he said again, "by any chance you have an alibi for last night?"

"An alibi?" I squeaked, all lust-filled thoughts fleeing from my head.

Alibi?

Rats.

I knew what that meant.

I watch *Law and Order, Law and Order SVU,* and *Law and Order Criminal Intent.* Is that all? I might be forgetting one, but that's understandable, given my circumstances.

Oh, and I watch *CSI.*

All that television meant I knew that cops didn't ask witnesses for alibis.

They asked suspects for them.

I was a murder suspect.

Check out Book #1 **Steamed: A Maid in LA Mystery**
Quincy Mac is a maid in LA—a maid who's accidently cleaned a murder scene. Now she's a murder suspect with only one option— find the real murderer before she ends up in jail for a crime she didn't commit. Quincy came to LA looking for fame and fortune. What she's found is infamy and misfortune. There's a killer out there, and Quincy's going to them… or die trying.

**Did you miss Quincy's second book,
Dusted: A Maid in LA Mystery?
*Here's an excerpt:***

I looked in the mirror and felt nothing but… horror.

Orange?

I have never owned any orange clothes, so I must have suspected all along that orange might not be my color, but looking in the mirror, I was positive—orange was soooo not my color.

Frankly, I don't know that orange is anyone's color. I mean, Tiny could keep calling it *rustic pumpkin* until the cows came home, but the fact of the matter was, my maid-of-honor dress was orange.

The other fact of the matter was, I looked like giant pumpkin.

"Quincy Mac, you are absolutely stunning." Tiny's voice was all breathless wonder.

The last two weeks she'd gone from wedding-itis to full blown wedding-fever. Everything she said was breathless.

Breathless wonder.

Breathless excitement.

Breathless anticipation.

"Breathe, Tiny," I reminded helpfully as I had countless times the last few weeks.

"You look so …" She stared to cry.

Breathless and crying. Those were Tiny's two modes of communication as her wedding day drew nearer.

I filled in the blank while I waited for her to compose herself.

You look so … *much like a pumpkin.*

You look so … *scary.*

You look so … *much like a tangerine.* Oh, who was I kidding, I was no tiny tangerine. I was a full-on navel orange.

I sucked in my baby-pooch and wished I'd thought to bring my body-sucker. Oh, I know that's not what it's actually called. These days people call them by their name brand. My Grandma Mac called hers a girdle and I don't think I ever saw her without it on. I'm pretty sure she was buried in it.

Note to my boys who would some day be in charge of burying me. Do not bury me in a body sucker.

"… so beautiful," Tiny finally managed.

I smiled and put all of Mr. Magee's acting classes to use by assuring her, "I love it, Tiny."

I didn't love it, but she did and that's all that mattered. Too many people forget that a wedding is the bride and groom's special day. It's the one day when thinking about yourself isn't the least bit selfish. If she wanted me to look like a pumpkin, then by gosh, I'd be a smiling pumpkin as I walked up that aisle.

Tiny's wedding was three weeks away. I had promised myself I'd do everything in my power to be sure it was perfect.

Heck, I'd even found out who murdered Mr. Banning in order to see to it I wasn't in jail for Tiny's wedding.

Okay, truth was, I didn't want to be in jail period. And since I'd accidently cleaned Mr. Banning's murder scene, I was the only viable suspect.

Yeah, that's right. I cleaned it. I washed and polished the murder weapon. I even steamed the footprints off the carpet.

My Uncle Bill went to jail for a crime he didn't commit. Eventually the authorities realized he was innocent. They let him out of prison, but he came out with a tattoo. Mac's do not get tattoos. Or go to prison for that matter.

I was determined not to go to jail and leave my boys, or miss Tiny's wedding…or get a tattoo. I just didn't think a tattoo would age well. I was thirty-eight, and though I avoided the sun as if I were a vampire rather than simply a fair-skinned woman, I knew that wrinkles would be forthcoming. And who wants to see a wrinkled tattoo unicorn, even if it was a declaration of my innocence?

No one, that's who.

Thankfully, I found the murderer. Of course, he tried to kill me to keep me quiet, but I grew up with brothers and three sons. I kicked him and made it count. I rescued myself before Cal came in to rescue me.

Detective Cal Parker, my new boyfriend. It felt so odd to use the word *boyfriend* when I was the mother of three teens and almost forty (sigh) but I hadn't come up with any better designation for him.

I must have sighed as I thought about my cute, hunky new boyfriend because Tiny laughed. "You're thinking about him, aren't you?"

"Him, who?" I asked, trying to sound as if I didn't have a clue what she was talking about.

"Him—Detective Sexy."

"I was thinking about your wedding."

Tiny laughed some more and humphed me in a way that I knew meant she wasn't buying it.

The phone rang. I sucked in my stomach as I walked across the room in my pumpkin colored dress. I picked up the phone. "Mac'Cleaners. We do it all and we're glad you called. How may I help you today?"

"Quincy, it's me," a woman's voice said.

I didn't need any more than that to know it was Theresa Maxwell. She was officially the worst employee Mac'Cleaners had ever had. To be honest, that whole cleaning-Mr.-Banning's-murder scene was her fault because she was supposed to be the one cleaning the dead-body house that day, but she'd called in sick. When an employee calls in sick, Tiny and I—as the business owners—step in and fill in for them. So Theresa is why I'd almost ended up in jail for a murder I didn't commit.

Theresa really was the worst employee ever, not just in an almost-sent-me-to-jail sort of way.

I'd like to fire her. I'd threatened to do just that, but I kept hoping she'd get better. Seriously, she couldn't get any worse. Although this call didn't bode well for the getting better and seemed to be pointing to worse. There was panic in her voice.

"What's up, Theresa?" I asked suspiciously.

"It's not what's up, it's what's down. I was dusting a painting at the Gifford's house and it fell. There's a tear in it now."

I'd seen the Gifford's house when I cleaned for Theresa a month ago. The last call of the day had been the dead body house, but the Gifford's house was part of her morning calls, which became my morning call when Theresa called in sick. I did not know much about art, but I knew enough to know their art was expensive. The Giffords lived in Hollywood Hills, an expensive part of town. I lived in Van George, where the cost of the houses sent my Pennsylvanian family into heart palpitations, but here in southern California was actually a mid-middle class sort of price.

"Oh…" I searched for a curse word I could use without being too crass or offending anyone. With three teenaged boys in the house, I really tried to watch myself.

"Boogers," I opted for. It was a pretty perfect curse word. Gross enough to get some umph out of, but not really offensive.

"I'm so sorry, Quincy," Theresa said. "I don't know what to do now."

"You'll have to call the Giffords and let them know what happened. Please take a picture of the damage with your cellphone, just to cross all our t's. I'll dot our i's by calling our insurance company to make a report. We've never had an accident like this happen, but please assure the Giffords we'll make it right."

"Okay," Theresa said and hung up.

I hit end on my phone and thumbed over to my contact list to look for our insurance company's number.

"Problems?" Tiny asked.

"Theresa," I managed.

"We're going to have to fire that girl," we said in sync.

I called the insurance company…

Check out Book #2, **Dusted: A Maid in LA Mystery**
Quincy's taking classes on writing and working on a script. She's taking care of her boys, wearing a pumpkin orange maid of honor dress for Tiny's wedding, and oh… she's got another case. Someone stole Mac'Cleaner clients' artwork, and Quincy's employee is under

suspicion. This is one LA maid who's got a lot on her plate in Holly Jacobs' second Maid in LA Mystery, Dusted.

Check out Book #3 **Spruced Up: A Maid in LA Novella**
Quincy Mac has faced a murder and an art thief. She's dealt with three teenaged boys on her own. She's even braved a brand new romance. But nothing she'd done in the past has prepared Quincy for this... she's heading home for Christmas! She's planning a quiet week with her family, but finds herself with another mystery to solve!

Join Quincy as she celebrates with her family and solves a mystery in a way that's perfect for the Christmas season!